TO THE GRAVE AND BACK

THE ACCIDENTAL REAPER URBAN FANTASY SERIES
BOOK 8

MISTY EVANS

Beach
Path
Publishing

To the Grave and Back, The Accidental Reaper Series, Book 8

©2026 Misty Evans

Print ISBN: 978-1-964028-35-4

Cover Art by Fanderclai Design www.fanderclai.com

Formatting by Beach Path Publishing, LLC

ONE

The dead never checked my calendar.

If they did, they'd know I'd already worked a twelve-hour shift at the vet clinic, cleaned up after three dogs with nervous stomachs, and pulled a squeaky toy out of a golden retriever's colon. But here I was, trudging through Shepherd's Rest cemetery at midnight, scythe humming against my back like it was auditioning for a rave.

Beside me, a white Papillon with bat-wing ears pranced over the frosted grass. Ghost gave a delicate sneeze, then fixed me with the kind of look that said *you'd better not screw this up tonight.* I swear, if she ever learns to talk, I'm doomed.

"You dragged me out of bed for this?" My witchy friend Aurora's voice carried an edge along with her faint Irish accent as she made her way toward me. Her breath puffed white in the chilly October air, and she had wrapped herself in a burnt orange wool coat and an attitude. She was a good friend and a regular backup for me when things went sideways during reaper work. "It's freezing out here. You owe me a pumpkin spice latte the size of my head."

"You owe me a hundred charms for letting you tag along," I shot back, good-naturedly. "This shade's supposed to be one of yours. Witch gone bad, unfinished spellwork, all that jazz. She died before her contract was up, hence why she's a shade and is trapped on our plane. I figured your people should be represented."

Aurora stopped a tombstone away. "My *people?*"

"You know what I mean."

She stepped over a chunk of busted stone path, her designer black boots super cute but sporting dangerous heels. "If it's who I think it is, she dabbled in blood rites above her abilities. No wonder she got stuck on this plane."

Ghost stopped dead ahead of us, hackles rising. Her fur shimmered, already blurring into the shape of the massive hound she became when it was time to cross a soul. My scythe vibrated harder, a low tremble of steel against leather.

Kill, it whispered.

Mist crept along the cracked gravestones, and I drew the blade, even though I hadn't yet located the witch's shade. "Showtime."

A shimmer of light flickered between the leaning gravestones like a candle flame caught in the wind. Then a figure bled into view—luminous, the hem of her crimson cape dragging through the frost, eyes glowing an unnatural, sickly green.

The shade clutched at phantom tools in her hands—a ritual athame, a bowl, herbs that weren't really there. Her lips moved in broken incantations, the words disjointed because of her unexpected separation from her physical body.

Aurora drew in a sharp breath. "Carmen Santos." Her tone carried a blend of disgust and pity. "Definitely a witch gone bad."

That confirmed the name Death had given me. I gripped the scythe tighter while the witch's shade swayed closer, eyes flicking to me like I was an intruder in her unfinished ritual. "What's with her eyes?" I asked. Most ghosts ran from me. They tended to like hanging around on the earthly plane. "Did she have green eyes like you while alive?"

Aurora stepped closer. "No, they were brown. She looks...possessed."

Just what I needed. I forced a smile. "Hi, Carmen. I'm Chloe, and I'm here to help you. All of us are." I gestured at Aurora and Ghost, who morphed into her psychopomp form. To the ghosts, she looked like a normal dog, full of kindness and wet kisses. It was a trick, like my blade appearing as something the noncompliant soul loved to get them to touch it. It made their crossing easier. "All you have to do is touch this, and Ghost here will give you a first-class ride to the afterlife. Smooth, painless, and absolutely no extra fees."

Ghost's low growl said she wasn't convinced it would be smooth or painless.

The shade's eyes narrowed, glowing hotter, her phantom athame slicing the air. "Get away," she hissed, the words jagged as broken glass. "I'm bound. I cannot cross."

I eased the blade up higher but stood my ground. "Bound, how? A spell gone sideways? Oath to a demon? Bad marriage contract?"

Aurora's brows drew tight. "Mother Goddess, she's telling the truth." She waved her hands through the air in front of us, fingers flicking. I could make out sparks of her magic showering over the shade. "She's tethered to something still here."

"Great." I blew out a sigh. "That's exactly what I want to hear at midnight in a graveyard."

Ghost cocked her head, ears pricking as though she heard something I didn't. A rumble built low in her chest, the sound vibrating against my bones. She fixed her gaze past the witch, toward the dark stretch of gravestones behind her.

"What is it, girl?"

The witch's muttering broke into a scream—high, keening, and wrong. Her shadow stretched across the frost like spilled ink, twisting, thickening. Then it ripped upward, tearing itself free of her ghostly form.

A second shape unfurled, tethered to her by cords of pale, spectral light. Fangs flashed in the dark, translucent claws curling as the figure resolved into something half-ghost, half-predator.

A vampire...shade?

He snarled, eyes gleaming with the hunger of the grave, his body blinking in and out of solidity. He wasn't supposed to exist—vampires were Undead, yes, but their souls followed different rules. I'd never seen one as a shade. Had he been turned the exact moment she died, their souls knotted together?

Aurora grimaced. "She's tangled up with that thing. She died tied to a vampire...who's, well, *dead*."

Nothing like this had been covered in my grim handbook "Fantastic." I rubbed the handle of the blade. "A two-for-one reap. That wasn't the assignment. Why didn't Death warn me?"

He probably hadn't known.

Ghost's protective growl deepened, her hackles bristling. She planted herself in front of me, teeth bared at the feral shade. Or I guess *shades*, plural.

The witch writhed, cords of spectral light binding her to the vampire now visible to me. Magic flew from her fingers, a spark or two landing on my scythe's otherworldly metal. Her voice was ragged as she shrieked, "I can't cross! The Ferryman waits at the river!"

Oh, the drama. "Yeah, okay, seen this before. It's called end-of-life jitters. Everybody thinks they're heading straight to heaven or hell, or Charon's waiting with a paddle boat."

Aurora had gone pale, her breath puffing in a fog. "No, Chloe." Her green eyes locked on the witch, unease radiating from every syllable. "She doesn't mean the River of the Dead."

"Then what?"

Aurora sighed and shook her head. "Nothing good."

My scythe thrummed. Heat licked up my arm, more violent than anything I'd felt before, like the weapon was trying to sear its way straight into my bones. My grim tattoo flamed to life, too.

"Easy there, Sparky." I tightened my grip, ignoring the searing pain. "You're supposed to help me reap souls, not roast me alive."

The witch shade shrieked as I shoved the blade forward, the edge barely kissing her arm. Her luminous form convulsed. Ghost clamped on her cape, and in the blink of an eye, they were both gone.

I would have been relieved except...

The vampire shade didn't go with her.

He let out a snarl, tether cords snapping as he wrenched free, ghostly fangs gleaming. His eyes fixed on me, hunger sparking there, and I had the very distinct feeling that I wasn't reaping him...

He was hunting me.

No time for niceties or etiquette. I lunged, driving the blade at him, angling for his chest. He twisted, faster than a ghost had any right to, and came at me with fangs bared.

The blade shuddered hard, singing in my hand. *Kill*, it demanded again.

I shoved it at the vampire shade's chest again. He met me head-on, spectral claws raking sparks across the steel, and emitted a pulse of magic. The force of it sent me skidding back on the frosted grass.

Ghost reappeared, slamming into him before he

could attack again. Her jaws closed on his shoulder, holding him long enough for me to thrust the blade into his ribs.

He shrieked—then *detonated*.

Not vanished like a typical soul crossing. His body blew apart in a burst of ash and shadow, scattering across the graves. The Veil—the in-between curtain that hung between the living world and the afterlife— rippled, shuddering like water after a massive stone drop. For one awful second, the air around us quivered and hissed.

Then it fell silent.

Aurora stared, wide-eyed. Ghost growled, ears flat, still braced as if waiting for something else to rush us.

I straightened, chest heaving, the shade's ashy remains clinging to my coat. I sure hoped the dry cleaner could get it out. "Well," I muttered. "Death's going to love my report on this."

TWO

The moment I stepped into the penthouse, exhaustion hit me like a sledgehammer.

Ghost bounded ahead, nails clicking on the polished floor, her giant ears perked as she sniffed her way toward the kitchen.

Pennyworth was at it again, bless his domestic, culinary heart. The scent of roasted garlic and herbs perked me up slightly, my mouth watering. I hadn't even had lunch, much less dinner.

Killion stood near the arm of the sofa, tall and composed as always, but the violet of his eyes sharpened when they met mine. His calm veneer didn't fool me— worry thrummed through our soul bond.

"Something happened," he murmured, bending to scratch Ghost's head as she danced around his legs. His hand lingered a moment, as if reassuring himself she was whole before his gaze returned to me. "I felt your anxiety."

I sighed, unhooking my scythe holder and dropping it, along with my jacket, onto the chair by the door. My palm still tingled from the earlier burn, but I dismissed the pain. Thanks to my grim and vampire abilities, it would heal fast.

Killion moved toward me, pressing a glass of wine into my hand before I could protest. His tie was missing, and the sleeves of his silver dress shirt were rolled up to his elbows. "Come and sit," he said.

I obeyed, sinking onto the sofa while Ghost padded to her bed near the fire, curling up with a huff. The flames cast warm light across the room, but the tension crawling over my skin didn't ease. I downed some of the wine and closed my eyes.

From his perch in the corner, Corvin screeched, "Kill!" It was the raven's favorite word—much like my scythe's—and one he delivered with unnerving timing.

"Not helpful," I muttered, which earned me a smug head-tilt and a click of his beak.

Killion settled beside me. He turned my upper body away from him gently, his fingers massaging my shoulders. "Tell me," he said.

I leaned into his touch, took another drink, and closed my eyes, enjoying the way his fingers kneaded the knots out of my neck. The wine was beginning to work its way through my system, but it wasn't enough to untangle the images in my head.

"This reap was supposed to be simple." I watched Ghost twirl in circles and then settle. "A witch shade named Carmen Santos. She botched a blood rite and died before her contract was up. I brought Aurora for backup."

Killion's fingers stalled. "What went wrong?"

"Carmen resisted, claiming she was bound."

"By her backfired magic?"

I shook my head. "She was tethered to a..." Reluctant to give up the massage, I did, anyway. I shifted so I could look him in the eye. "A vampire."

Nothing changed in his posture or expression, but I felt him draw back internally. "Are you sure?"

"Very. Not living-Undead. Dead-dead. Which, for the record, should not be a thing, but it was a vampire shade, Killion. He was tethered to her like a shadow stitched into her soul."

My husband's dark brows crashed together. "Impossible."

"That's what I thought. Vampires don't leave shades. I've never seen one. But this wasn't just a flicker or an echo. He was..." I struggled to find the word for it. "Feral. Half-ghost, half-hungry predator. Fangs and all."

Ghost let out a low groan from her bed, as if the memory disturbed her sleep.

I took another gulp of wine before continuing. "The witch screamed she couldn't cross because the Ferryman was waiting. And when I forced her to the blade, she went, but the vampire?" My voice dropped. "He didn't. I had to fight him, and when I finally reaped him, he didn't cross cleanly. He *exploded*, sending ashes everywhere." I brushed at my shirt, finding some of the remains on it.

"And the Veil did this weird ripple thing. I've never seen it do that before."

A log snapped in the fireplace, punctuating my words. Killion didn't move, but through our bond, his unease hit me like a cold wave.

From his perch, Corvin gave a rough laugh that sounded like gravel in a blender. "Boom," he croaked. Then added with eerie cheer, "Extra crispy!"

I pinched the bridge of my nose. "I'm living in a grim comedy."

Killion shot the raven a flat look. Corvin only fluffed his feathers.

My husband stood and paced in front of the hearth. The flames threw sharp lines across his handsome face and midnight black hair, making him look even more severe. "Vampires do not leave shades," he said. "They cannot exist. Which means we have a problem."

"It was messy, but I handled it." I laid my head on the back of the sofa. "I'm sure the Ferryman thing was probably the witch's brain scrambling metaphors. River Styx, Charon—take your pick. And the vampire shade is just an oddity. We've seen plenty of those lately."

Killion fixed me with a look that said I'd missed the obvious. "The witch wasn't mixing myths. There are stories of the Ferryman in many ancient texts. He's the one who crossed between realms without Death's sanction."

Great. My boss wasn't big on entities like that. They upended Universal balance and threw Soul Management

Group, our employer, into chaos. "The Ferryman is real? You're sure?"

"I have no direct proof." Killion ran a hand through his dark hair, frustration crackling down our bond. "But if shades are invoking his name, if they're afraid, then something has stirred him, or his memory. Either possibility is dangerous."

From his perch, Corvin clicked his beak. "Ferryman," he echoed in a sing-song croak. "Pay the toll."

I groaned. "Death is going to hate this."

Pennyworth stuck his head out of the kitchen doorway. "Are you ready for dinner, Master?"

"Can you eat?" Killion asked me.

I can *always* eat, and I was starving after the cemetery. Coming to my feet, I swirled the wine left in my glass, staring into the dark red depths like it might offer an easier answer. "Absolutely. I'll send my report to Death in the morning and let him figure it out."

Killion's head snapped up, eyes reflecting the firelight. "Tomorrow is too late." His voice had an urgent, dangerous edge. "If the Ferryman is involved, if there are vampire shades and they're erupting into ash instead of crossing, this is not something you file and forget. Someone's messing with the Veil."

I waved him off, though unease prickled the back of my neck. "You make it sound like he's going to show up at our front door if I don't file a report immediately."

Killion stepped to me, cupping my jaw with surprising gentleness for the steel in his voice. "Chloe, I need you to hear me. You had a witch shade claiming the

Ferryman was waiting for her on the other side, and she was tethered to a vampire shade. None of that is normal. It's a warning. Something is wrong. You must tell Death tonight. Not tomorrow."

"Ugh," I muttered, letting him tug me to the dining room, where Pennyworth was loading the long table with his latest concoction. It smelled divine. "Fine, as soon as we're done eating. I can't face him on an empty stomach."

Roasted chicken glazed with honey and rosemary made my mouth water. A casserole dish held garlic mashed potatoes smoother than any potion Aurora ever brewed, and there were green beans tossed with almonds. My stomach growled loud enough to wake Ghost. She trotted over, and Pennyworth served her some meat in her dish.

"You spoil us," I told him as I snagged a spoonful of potatoes.

He inclined his head in that dignified way of his. "One tries." Then he disappeared back into the kitchen.

After ash and cold grave air, the meal was heaven. I closed my eyes with a groan. "If I die on a reap, I want you to promise Pennyworth will cater the wake."

Killion refilled my wine and sat at the head of the table. He arched a brow, slicing into the chicken and feeding me a bite with a practiced hand. "You're not dying on a reap."

"Still. Contingency planning."

We ate, Ghost returning to her bed after she'd had her fill, and Corvin finally falling silent. For a few minutes, it almost felt normal—just a married couple, a weird menagerie of pets, and a meal that would make Michelin weep.

By the time I set down my fork, warmth had replaced the chill of Shepherd's Rest. I stretched, yawning. "Okay. Shower, pajamas, maybe a cheesy baking show, and then I'll file the report. Promise."

Killion's eyes narrowed in that way that said he didn't believe me for a second.

Before I could make my escape, the temperature in the room plummeted. The fire guttered, shadows stretching long and sharp across the walls. Ghost jerked awake and jumped to her feet, while Corvin flapped and screeched, "Kill! Kill!"

And then Death was there, standing in the middle of our living room as if he'd stepped straight out of the grave. Tonight, his hair was a rich chestnut color, and it hung to his shoulders. He wore a tight T-shirt and ripped jeans over a pair of black boots. "We need to talk, Grave Girl."

"Great," I muttered, dragging a hand down my face. "I guess the shower has to wait."

Death marched into the dining room, snagged my wine glass, and polished off its contents. "I felt a ripple in the Veil. Naturally, I assumed it involved you. Explain."

I jerked my glass out of his hand and set it back on the table. "Good evening to you, too. And I'm offended that you jumped to that conclusion."

Killion bristled, muscles taut. "You will show respect for her when in this house. *My* house."

Death didn't even glance at him.

I pinched the bridge of my nose. "You think I caused the ripple."

"Ground Zero was Shepherd's Rest, so yes," he countered. "Report."

"Seriously?" I gestured at the now-empty wine glass, the fire, the perfect night I'd been trying to salvage. "I was two seconds from a shower and maybe half an episode of Bake-Off. I promise to write up the details and send them to you within the hour, okay?"

His expression didn't shift, but the fire in the hearth banked. "Just spit it out. What did you do?"

As if reading my mind, Killion refilled my glass and launched into the short version. "You assigned her a witch shade who claimed the Ferryman was waiting for her on the other side. She was tethered to a vampire shade. The witch crossed, and the vampire exploded into ashes. The Veil rippled oddly."

Death actually blinked, which was almost more alarming than the ripple. "What in the dead realms are you talking about?

I repeated what Killion had volunteered, then shrugged. "I have no idea what caused the ripple, but I assume it's tied to the witch and her vampire."

He dragged out a chair and sat. Pennyworth appeared and placed a table setting in front of him, but Death wasn't interested in food. Unusual, for sure, but it was alarming to see my boss speechless for once.

"What does it mean?" I asked. "Is the Ferryman a real thing?"

He rubbed a hand down his face. "Oh, he's real, all right."

I waited for him to go on, but he didn't. He slammed his hands on the table, rose to his feet, and shook his head. "I'll get back to you."

With that, he disappeared.

I let out a relieved sigh. "Time for that shower."

My husband picked up our wine glasses. "Would you like help scrubbing your back?"

I grinned. "I'm so tired, I think I need help scrubbing everything."

He handed me the wine and took my elbow to steer me toward the master bath. "I'm at your service, wife."

Everything in me tingled. "I think I'll skip the cooking show."

We passed through the bedroom and into the gorgeous bath. He started the shower and arched his brow at me. "Why would you do that?"

I set down the glass and wrapped my arms around his neck. "Because I think I can find more interesting entertainment right here."

He kissed me long and deep, and then began undressing me. "It's not every day I have to compete with reality TV."

I chuckled, and then caught my breath when his fangs grazed the sensitive skin of my neck. "Oh, believe me, there's absolutely no competition."

THREE

By nine the following morning, I'd traded my scythe and robes for coffee and dog hair.

The clinic smelled like disinfectant and wet fur, which was basically eau de parfum for my soul. Sylvie— saint, office manager, and friend—already had the phone tucked against one ear while she typed like a demon.

"Morning, boss," she called, not looking up as a carrier on the counter emitted the sound of a blender full of bees. "You've got Mr. Finley's geriatric shepherd in Room Two, a parakeet with a wheeze in Three, and Mrs. Laramie's rat in One who is, and I quote, 'possessed by Satan and also maybe chewing the drywall.' Sign here, here, and... don't forget the vaccine cooler."

Ghost trotted at my heels, dainty as a debutante and twice as confident. I snagged a lab coat, scrawled my signature on three forms I refused to read before caffeine, and set them on the edge of her desk. "If the rat starts speaking Latin, you're calling a priest."

"I already called two," she said with a crooked grin. "They hung up."

Room Two's shepherd was a sweetheart with a grizzled muzzle and a heart murmur I could feel with two fingers. I stroked his ears, let Ghost sit like a calm little support companion at the exam table's foot, and adjusted his meds for comfort over miracles. Mr. Finley clutched his hat and nodded along, eyes soft. This part of my job was a mix of fix-what-you-can and hold-what-you-can't.

The parakeet in Three wheezed like bagpipes under a truck, but antibiotics and a heat lamp would help. I handed off instructions and hustled to One, where Mrs. Laramie's rat tried to remove my thumb out of pure spite.

"I'm billing you for that," I told him, prying his tiny demon jaws off my glove.

I'd just finished with them and washed my hands when a cat I didn't recognize padded past the open door. It was a sleek, silver tabby, with dainty feet that didn't quite touch the tile. I started to tell Sylvie she had a runaway client when it walked straight through the trash can.

"Okay," I muttered.

Ghost sniffed and barked.

I stuck my head out. "Um, Sylvie?"

She peeked down the corridor, hand over the phone's mouthpiece. "Yes?"

"Is it a full moon?"

"Not for another week," she said, returning to her phone call.

The silver tabby glanced between us with eyes like polished coins. It flicked its tail once at Ghost and vanished into thin air, leaving an odd ripple behind.

My skin tightened. The Veil-ripple memory from the previous night flashed in my mind.

I meandered to the front, Ghost on my heels. There were only two patients in the waiting room, and I pretended to be reviewing their charts. When Sylvie finished her call, she looked up and frowned. "You okay? You're white as Ms. Downing's Persian."

"I'm fine," I lied, lowering my voice. "But have you seen any *odd* pets running around unattended?"

One brow shot up. "No. Should I be on the lookout?"

I nodded.

The bell over the front door jingled. Aurora swept in on a gust of October air, scarf fluttering, and cheeks pink. Andy trailed behind her, hands shoved in his jacket pockets, shoulders set in the determined way of someone trying not to scowl. Ghost gave a wag for Aurora and a sympathetic blink for Andy.

"Can we talk to you for a moment in private?" Aurora asked.

I led them to the breakroom at the rear of the building. "What's up?"

She pulled off her gloves. "Have you noticed any unusual spectral activity?"

I hooked a thumb at the corridor. "A phantom tabby just took a stroll through my trash can."

She winced. "That's what I was afraid of."

Andy's jaw flexed. "So even your clinic isn't safe."

"Safe from what, exactly?"

"Spirits aren't staying on the other side," Aurora said. "My graveyard is like Times Square this morning. The dead are crossing back through the Veil to hang out."

Andy huffed. "At least you two can see them." His bitterness wasn't loud, but it was there.

In the spring, he'd contracted a supernatural parasitic illness. To kill the parasites, Killion had needed to use his dragon fire to burn them out of Andy's system. Unfortunately, it had also destroyed his shifter magic. He could no longer turn into a wolf. He was just...human now.

To have magic and then lose it was worse than death for most supernaturals. He was depressed most days, and we all understood why.

I bumped my shoulder against his. "Trust me, the paperwork involved in being a reaper is the real monster, and rogue ghosts require a lot of paperwork."

"That's not—" He cut himself off, mouth flattening.

Aurora sent me a look. *Tread carefully.*

I nodded. *Noted.*

I led them to an exam room where we'd have more privacy and shut the door. Ghost followed and hopped onto the chair like a small, furry person who wanted to be included in our conversation.

Aurora set her tote on the counter, the contents clinking. Usually, she carried herbs, tinctures, and a thermos of tea that tasted like grass. Her own portable apothecary. Andy hovered near the sink, hands still in his pockets, glare fixed on the floor.

"So," I said, perching on the stool. "Remember how the witch mentioned the Ferryman last night?" Aurora nodded. "Killion says he isn't just a myth. There are mentions in a bunch of old texts about a being who crosses between realms without Death's sanction."

Aurora's mouth thinned. "Aye. I was up until three, poring through grimoires. There are notes of a tide-taker, a creature who exists at the edge of rivers that aren't really rivers. Souls that owe something have to go to him. He shows up on our plane when the balance breaks."

I rubbed my palm, where the scythe-burn had left a phantom heat. "Death showed up in our living room after I got home. He felt the ripple in the Veil and naturally assumed I caused it. Wanted my full report right then."

Andy's head came up. "Glad he's your boss and not mine."

"Yep, he dropped right in, drank my wine, and complained. But he was...rattled. He'll deny it, but he was."

Aurora's mouth screwed up in thought. "And your scythe?"

"Humming when it shouldn't." I flexed my fingers. "It burned me last night."

Ghost stared at the door like someone with treats might come through. In the corridor, I heard JR's voice as he arrived for work and received his first case from Sylvie.

"The witch's blood rites," Aurora said, flipping through her notebook. "They weren't simple bindings. Carmen Santos was playing with tethering magic—

outlawed a century ago. Designed to tie a soul to a power source. A patron. A... creature." She swallowed. "She hooked herself to a vampire before she died—by accident or intention. It might have dragged a fragment of him with her. But that still shouldn't make him a shade."

"Yet it did." Andy's voice was sharp. "And you fought it, and the Veil rippled, and Death came running. Meanwhile, I can't shift, can't help, can't—" He bit off the rest.

I met his gaze. "You being here helps."

He rolled his eyes.

"I mean it," I said in my no-nonsense, I'm-in-charge voice. "So stop with the pity party."

He almost smiled.

Ghost's hackles rose without warning. She continued to stare past us at the door, and the hair on my arms prickled. I cracked open the door and peered into the hall.

A dog was there, a huge, gray, deep-chested thing with eyes like old iron. A hound, but not one of our patients. Its paws didn't touch the floor either. It lifted its head and howled, and the sound went through the clinic like a bell tolling.

The living animals responded in a chorus of barks, yowls, and screeches. Sylvie stuck her head out from the desk. "Uh. Doc? What was that?"

"It just walked through the wall," Aurora muttered. She moved to my side and whispered a protection charm. "They're gathering."

"Gathering for what?" Andy asked.

I hustled toward the hound, but it blinked out and was gone.

"What was that?" JR asked, coming out of Room Three.

I hurried to the front, where our patients were in an uproar. Outside the front windows, something antlered glided past—tall as the doorframe. A stag.

I forced myself to breathe. "Nope, nope, nope."

A client opened the door from outside at that exact second, and the stag drifted through with him. The man shivered and looked around, seeming confused, then shrugged and hustled in his schnauzer like we weren't hosting a spectral parade.

Aurora's hand found my sleeve and squeezed. "Chloe...?"

"I know." My voice came out thin. I cleared my throat. The comment didn't make sense, like saying you're fine when you're not. But it was all I could come up with. "I know."

Andy's eyes were bright and bleak. "Tell me this isn't something really big."

I pasted on my vet smile—the one that said we're going to fix this, even if I had no idea how. The same smile I used on the shepherd's owner earlier. "Whatever it is, we'll handle it."

Aurora's fingers tightened on my sleeve, her voice barely above a whisper. "How exactly? What are we going to do?"

The clinic was supposed to be the safe part of my life. Lately, even that wasn't true. "The one thing I don't want to."

Andy's brows lifted. "Which is?"

I grimaced. "I have to talk to Death again."

Ghost gave a sharp bark, either of agreement or in sympathy.

FOUR

After hours, the clinic always felt like a church after the congregation had gone. It was quiet, scuffed, and holy in the way that only ordinary work can be.

I flipped the sign to CLOSED and returned to my office to wrestle the last of my charts into the system.

A few minutes later, Sylvie tapped on my doorframe with a manila folder pinched like a hot potato. "Your Weird Animal Log," she said, lips twitching. "I started it as a joke at lunch, but it grew enough that I think you have a serious problem."

I took the file. The first page was neatly typed because Sylvie is the consummate office manager. I'm lucky she's so good at her job, and she knows all about the supernatural world and about me being a grim.

9:18 a.m. Spectral tabby (silver). Phase-walked through trash can; ignored litter box.

10:42 a.m. Translucent hound (gray). Howled. All live dogs sang the song of their people.

11:07 *a.m. Antlered... thing. Possibly stag. Walked through Mr. Chen. He says he's fine, but he's taking the schnauzer to church now.*

1:33 *p.m. Two cats weaving around ankles.*

3:20 *p.m. Owl perched on the reception computer and judged me.*

There were another dozen entries. "I love your notes." I laughed because it felt safer than the alternative, which was screaming. "Hopefully, this isn't going to be a daily thing."

"What if it is?" She leaned against the jamb, searching my face. "Anything I can do? Besides updating my résumé to include 'ghost traffic controller?'"

"You've done plenty. Go home. Hug Silas and your babies." They had a dog and a cat. "I sent Death a message, and I'm waiting, like usual, for him to get back to me. There's not much you can do on that front unless you've got him on speed dial."

"Please." She rolled her eyes. "He stood up for me with SMG, but I think he felt I then betrayed him because I ditched them to work for you. We aren't exactly on speaking terms these days. Lock up behind you?"

"Always."

She pushed off the frame, then paused. "If you need me for—" She made a vague circular motion that encompassed the entire place. "I'm not saying I'll be useful, but I'll bring snacks."

"Bless you," I said. Ghost barked. "Ghost and I are always up for bakery items. She likes sprinkles."

"You got it." She saluted with her pen and vanished

down the hall. A minute later, the chime above the door sounded, then fell silent. I was alone with the hum of the fridge in the breakroom, the soft tick of the clock on the wall, and Ghost dropped into her bed under my desk and started snoring like a furry metronome.

I typed the last line of my day's notes. The message I'd sent Death after Aurora and Andy left still showed as delivered, unread. Typical. I shoved the weird animal log into my bag with the rest of the paperwork I was going to tackle at home and reached for the light.

"I've been looking for you," Death said, materializing between my chair and the cabinets like he'd been filed under D all day.

I pivoted slowly. "Looking for me? I'm here if I'm not reaping souls, which you're aware of. If you answered your messages, you'd know what I've been facing today."

Tonight, he'd chosen a black coat over a simple shirt and trousers. "A council has been convened."

"What council?"

He held up a hand. No humor. No patience. None of his tacky accents. "The ripple you created triggered an emergency session at SMG. The witch's soul has not reached intake. You need to present what you know to this emergency council."

"*Created*," I echoed flatly. "I didn't create anything."

"Are you sure about that? You were there when it happened." Under stress, his go-to was usually snide comments and flippant movie quotes. The fact he was so solemn told this had definitely gotten under his skin.

"And your report mentioned a vampire shade and the Ferryman. A triple threat."

I slumped back into my chair, stared at the ceiling tile where someone had once drawn a smiley face in pencil. "You know I hate public speaking."

"Bring your robes and the blade."

While I don't like carrying them, I do. The robes rarely see the light of day or the gloom of night because they're heavy and scratchy, but I like to have them in case I need them. "Is there an option where I quit and open a cat café?"

"No."

I sighed, dug under the desk for my duffel bag containing said grim reaper tools, and slid my compact scythe into its leather holster with a practiced, resentful motion. As I slung the strap over my shoulder, I thumbed a quick text to Killion. *Death is dragging me to SMG for a council meeting. Don't wait up. Love you.*

The bond between us hummed warm and fierce. Three dots appeared, and then, *Be careful. I'm awake. Call if you need me.*

"Ready?" Death asked.

"No," I said, standing. "But let's get this over with."

He made a dismissive flick of his fingers. Ghost sprang to her feet, shook once, and in the span of that motion swelled from delicate Papillion to massive psychopomp.

The clinic peeled away. The world blinked, and we shot through several dimensions, skimming the in-between, where souls sometimes linger.

While I'd visited Soul Management Group on several occasions, I'd never been in the council chamber. The black marble floor was so polished that it reflected our images back to me. Candles suspended in clear glass globes burned without smoke, their light cold as stars.

The gallery held a dozen robed figures, faces shadowed, all turned toward the dais where five councilors sat beneath a plaque that read Soul Management Group.

Ghost growled softly. I scratched behind her ear, more for me than for her. "It's okay, girl."

A silver-braided woman rapped her knuckles on the arm of her chair. "Let's begin," she intoned. "Death and Chloe Frost are added to the attendance. Mei Han is absent pending her review status."

My gaze flicked to the empty seat in the second tier, the one that should hold Mei's impossible poise. Once upon a time, she'd been SMG's CEO. Then she'd decided doing the wrong thing for the right reasons would wash clean. The whole Silas Mercer curse debacle back in April said otherwise. "What do you need from me?" I asked.

The council members looked at me in shock. Death took one step to my right, as if distancing himself from my lack of manners. "There are protocols," he muttered under his breath. "Don't speak until you're spoken to."

Yeah, not happening. "Sorry, but I have a life that I'd like to get back to."

"We have your preliminary report," said Silver-braid in a tight, annoyed tone. "Add to it. Shepherd's Rest. The witch, Carmen Santos. The...attachment. Expand on the details."

I took a deep breath and gave them the blow-by-blow. The witch's resistance. Her exact words. The way the vampire shade unspooled from her. The blade burning my palm, the Ferryman's name, the explosion that hadn't been like any crossing I'd ever experienced.

A thin man to her left leaned forward, fingers steepled. "Your weapon reacted violently?"

"My weapon reacts sometimes when souls are being difficult," I said. "It reacted more than normal this time, but it did its job when I forced the witch to cross. The vampire exploded—not the scythe's fault."

"And the Veil *rippled*?" he asked.

"Yes."

Murmurs seethed like snakes under the council's breath. An archivist-looking councilor spoke, his eyes gleaming with that particular academic hunger that put knowledge before people. I'd seen plenty of his kind during my college years. "For the record, your scythe is the First Blade, correct?"

"First, as in... prototype?" one of the robed figures in the gallery asked.

"First." The word rolled around on his tongue, as if he were savoring it. "The blade carried by the original reaper—the one we call Grim Zero." He pointed at me.

A dozen gazes landed on me.

I lifted a hand. "Hey." At Death's menacing growl, I dropped it. "Honestly, I didn't even realize that the scythe was the original, but it makes sense. I'm the first reaper reincarnated, and my scythe is the original blade."

"Grim Zero's blade," he emphasized, as if I hadn't spoken, "is inextricable from the Veil. It is a key and a seam. If it is compromised—"

"Compromised?" I cut in.

"Yes, compromised. It is malfunctioning, which could damage the fabric between realms. What you experienced may be the first wobble in a failure cascade."

"Wobble," I repeated. I was starting to sound like Corvin. "A cascade of what, exactly?"

Another councilor, a woman with black ink swirling like tide marks up her throat, spoke. "I recommend a decommission. Destroy it before it tears more."

My scythe vibrated at my back, not a hum but a throat-deep snarl. Ghost's head came up, eyes snapping to me.

My insides tensed. Decommission my blade? "I don't think that's necessary. It was just a hiccup, and I'm fine."

The blade shrieked. The sound ripped through the chamber like metal dragged across metal. We all flinched. The holster leather burned hot enough to smoke. The obsidian under my boots spider-webbed with a crack that raced toward the dais.

The candles flickered. A few of the robed figures recoiled. At least one swore. The scythe leaped into my hand, and for a second, I thought it meant to strike on its own. "*Kill,*" it howled.

"Enough," Death commanded. The blade's scream

pitched down to a sullen buzz, then to silence. The room bent toward us.

My heart hammered. I met the archivist's gaze as I kept a firm grip on the handle. "It's a bit sensitive, is all," I said sweetly. To the blade, I mentally said, *Behave*!

Death stepped forward. "The scythe is not the problem." He sent me a quick glance. "Nor is its bearer."

A low hiss of disapproval shivered across the benches.

"The problem is what waits in the dark," he went on. "Oblivion wants through the Veil. The Ferryman acts as his hand. You can posture over rules and procedures while the seam splits, or you can support the grim reaper with the only blade that can stitch it shut."

"Oblivion?" I muttered. "What—who—is that?"

His lips barely moved as he responded. "I'll explain later."

All those gazes burned into me again. My spine straightened, even as my stomach tried to pack a bag and leave my body.

Silver-braid folded her hands. "What are you proposing?"

"I'm not *proposing*," Death said. "I am informing. Chloe and I will investigate the vampire shade and the Veil ripple. We will report only what is necessary. And you will not touch her blade."

"Overreach," the ink-throated councilor called out. "You cannot simply claim—"

He looked at her. Just looked. Shadows gathered like

bruises at the edge of the room. She shut her mouth with an audible click.

"Meeting adjourned," Death said, which was not at all how meetings worked here, and then the world folded like a paper crane again, and I fell through its belly.

We landed in the penthouse living room. The shift made my knees loose. Ghost shook once and shrank, fur shimmering as she settled back into her three-pound puppy self. She trotted off to her water dish. She was used to interdimensional travel. Me, not so much.

Killion came out of his chair in front of the fireplace. "Is everything all right?"

I set my bag on the coffee table with a thunk and caressed my scythe. "Not exactly, but here we are."

Death's gaze slid down me, cataloging my standard work clothes—tan pants, a loose blouse, and a button-down top with cartoon cats and dogs on it. "You need to change."

I blinked. "Excuse me?"

"Dress for a fight."

"Why?" I planted my hands on my hips. "Where are we going?"

He was already fading at the edges, the room's light bending the way it did sometimes when he moved between worlds. "Meet me at the cemetery," he said, tossing a glance at Killion. "Bring Fang Boy."

And then he was gone, the air snapping with the faintest taste of hoarfrost.

I stared at the space where he'd vanished, then at

Killion, then at Ghost, who tilted her head like a question mark.

"Fine," I said, my pulse skipping from dread and adrenaline. "Looks like another night at the cemetery."

Killion's mouth curved, humorless. "I'll get my coat. Fang Boy hates to keep Death waiting."

FIVE

Mist clung low to the ground, curling around the crooked stones of the cemetery. The cool October air smelled damp and mossy, settling heavily in my lungs.

Ghost padded ahead of us, her white coat lit under a pale, reluctant moon. Every few steps, she paused to sniff before pressing forward again.

I shifted the strap of my scythe holster. The blade pushed hard against my spine, propelling me along. "Is it me," I asked, "or does Shepherd's Rest look like it skipped straight to post-apocalypse chic?"

"Not just you." Killion scanned the shadows like every headstone was going to sprout fangs. His violet eyes glowed. "The mist seems...unnatural."

Behind us, Death appeared, his boots crushing the grass. "The Veil here has always been thin. Now it's..." He squinted as he stopped on my right side. "Opaque."

Like a dog tugging on its leash, my blade yanked

against the holster, nearly wrenching free. I grabbed the hilt and heat scorched my palm again. "*Kill*," it hissed in my mind.

Killion glanced at me, having heard the scythe through our link. "Your blade is exceptionally reactive tonight."

He'd listened in on the council meeting through our bond and learned how they wanted to decommission it because it might make things worse. "Guess it wants to play with the Veil?"

Killion shook his head. "If the steel is tied to the Veil, it should strengthen its resistance to whatever is trying to come through." He focused on Death. "Correct?"

"Could go either way," my boss said. "That's why Chloe and I are investigating."

The scythe shivered and rang like a tuning fork. "Can SMG really decommission it? What will they do? Take it apart? Destroy it?"

Ghost barked once, short and sharp, as if angry at the very thought. Death walked toward the edge of some bushes along the back of a mausoleum. "Any of that. All of it."

The blade shrieked again. I held it to my chest. "I won't let them," I promised it, "but you have to cooperate with me."

Killion's hand brushed my elbow. "Where did you reap the witch last night?"

My palm was red, skin prickling like I'd grabbed the wrong side of an iron. I pointed. "Over there."

Before any of us could move, a sound drifted through

the mist—low and distant, like the scrape of chains against stone. Then a steady, rhythmic *splash, splash, splash,* like oars pushing through water.

I froze. "Tell me you heard that."

Death tilted his head, eyes narrowing.

Killion nodded grimly. "The Ferryman?"

We all glanced around but saw no visual evidence of him. "Okay. So what's the Ferryman's deal?" I asked Death. "And don't tell me he's moonlighting from Greek mythology, because I really don't have the energy for Charon jokes right now. At the Council meeting, you mentioned Oblivion. Who is that?"

He fixed his attention on the deeper dark between the mausoleum and the bushes. "The Ferryman is not Greek, and he is not a myth."

"Then what is he?"

"Oblivion's hand." Death folded his arms over his massive chest, continuing to stare at the shadowed space. "Oblivion isn't a being of physical form, but an energy older than gods, older than the Veil itself. A devourer. Where life and death form a circle, he's the void outside it, hungering for endings without beginnings."

I shivered at the term 'devourer,' even though it conjured an image of the old Pac-Man game. "So...he's a cosmic garbage disposal?"

Death grunted. "The Ferryman comes when Oblivion stirs. He doesn't carry souls to their rightful ends. He drags them into nothingness. Into an unmaking of sorts."

Killion produced his own weapon, a dagger that

flashed silver in the dim light. "And vampires? We walk the line between the living and the dead. Does that make us targets?"

"Yes." Death's answer was without sympathy. "Vampires were never meant to exist in the balance. You're a loophole in the grand plan. You, especially, with your otherworldly dragon heritage. With the Veil thinning, the Ferryman may find your kind easy prey."

I glanced sidelong at Killion, whose jaw locked. The memory of the vampire shade twisted my stomach.

Death moved ahead of us, raising a hand. Shadows peeled back like fabric tugged from a seam. His magic made the hairs on the back of my neck stand up.

A hairline tear between two leaning stones appeared out of nowhere. It pulsed, subtle but insistent, as though it had a heartbeat. The air around us dropped ten degrees, and Ghost whined, not even sniffing at the edges of it.

"What's that?" I asked.

More of Death's magic unfurled, and the tear quivered. "The rift."

"Lovely," I whispered. "Our very own supernatural wormhole."

"This is more than a simple rip between dimensions." His voice dropped a notch, and I watched as ghostly figures swam past the opening. "It's a wound. The tethering magic you cut last night has strained the Veil, but Oblivion is pressing from the other side. His energy seeks to crawl through."

My scythe thrashed in my grip again, and the tattoo

on my chest warmed. I doubled over, clutching the hilt and sucking in a breath. "Why is my blade reacting like this? It's never—"

Death's eyes flicked to me, unreadable. "Because it remembers. It was the first seam. It knows how to close this type of wound. But it can also tear it wider."

"Oh, good," I panted. "A double-edged sword."

No one laughed at my pun.

The rift pulsed, and a tiny earthquake rippled through the ground. A gash of earth opened up, forming a thin crater. The rumble grew, and several headstones disappeared as the crooked rupture expanded.

Killion hauled me back just as another jagged fissure opened near my feet.

Then something clawed its way through—half-formed, half-not. It looked vaguely human, but its face seemed melted from the cheeks down. Its arms were too long, the fingers curved into claws.

It shrieked and lunged.

Ghost leapt at the same time, intercepting it with a snarl, but her teeth passed through its flesh. Killion struck, slashing at it, and the creature howled, but instead of bleeding, it split into smoke. In the next second, the tendrils reformed.

"Great," I said, raising the scythe. "Another noncompliant."

The blade roared as I swung. The edge met the shade-like spirit's chest, and for a moment, it froze. It screamed and then exploded into black mist. The mist didn't disperse—it seeped back into the rift, sucked into it like smoke into a vent.

The rift pulsed again. I swear it seemed almost... smug.

Death's face was carved in shadow. "He's testing the seam by sending shades through."

I pressed a shaking hand to my chest, breath ragged. Ghost came to stand beside me. Killion steadied me, his palm warm on my arm. "What can we do to close it?"

Death poured magic into the crevices. "This is only the beginning. If Oblivion is pushing through, the Ferryman will be here before we know it."

I thought of the sound of the oars. "Are you sure he's not already?"

The cracks in the ground closed up. Death glanced at my scythe. "Bring it here."

He gestured for me to follow him to the rip. Then, he held out his hand for the blade. A part of me didn't want to share, but I did, placing the hilt in his palm.

He shut his eyes for a brief moment, and the scythe shivered, then began to hum. A glow emanated from the steel, and the light seemed to reach for the opening.

Before it could touch it, however, my blade jerked from Death's grip and landed in mine.

My boss opened his eyes and glared at me. "What?" I said. "I can't help it if it likes me better than you."

He narrowed his eyes. "Touch the rip with it."

Honestly, I was leery of getting anywhere near that split. The scythe seemed to be, too. As I walked forward and held it out, the scythe shot a fiery blaze up my hand and into my arm. I cried out and dropped it.

Killion and Death were both beside me in an instant. The blade quivered on the ground. Killion immediately covered my burned palm with his and sent healing magic into it. I leaned against him, blinking away the tears.

Death frowned, examining my weapon. The glow along the scythe's edge guttered like a dying star. His jaw clenched, the shadows around him tightening. "This is bad. Very bad."

"What's wrong with it?"

"It refuses to cooperate," he said finally. "It won't obey anyone—not even me. That makes it both our greatest weapon and our greatest liability. I hate to say it, but we may have to take it to Smudgy and let them do what they said—decommission it."

The words sank into me like a concrete block. My palm still throbbed despite Killion's magic. The scythe seemed to cry with a defiance that I didn't understand, and the Veil pulsed harder, faster.

I swallowed and stared at the rift, at the ghostly shimmers waiting just beyond it. The Ferryman. Oblivion. Endings without beginnings. "I can't let them take my weapon. We need a way to fix this. What can we do?"

Death's eyes stayed fixed on the rift. "Contain it. Delay it. Pray the seam holds long enough for us to find answers."

"Pray?" I snorted. "That's your plan?"

"It's not a plan." His voice boomed in the quiet cemetery. "It's survival." His gaze flicked to the scythe. "That weapon is an original. It's tied to the universe. If it refuses to cooperate, it may force your hand to do what must be done. Whatever we do, we have to be prepared for the Ferryman. For Oblivion."

Killion's arm tightened around me. His voice was steel, his magic blanketing me. "If the Ferryman comes for any of us, he'll have a battle on his hands."

The rift pulsed again—hungry, patient, waiting.

Hesitantly, I picked up the blade. This time, it settled into my palm like usual. It was a reminder of who I was and what I'd been reborn to do. My scythe might be stubborn, the Veil might be cracking, and the Ferryman might be rowing straight for us, but I wasn't about to hand over my blade or my job to anyone.

"Look," I said, staring at the darkness spilling through the seam. "If the Veil's wobbling, we figure out how to stitch it, block it, whatever. But first we find out *why* Oblivion wants through."

The rift gave a long, shuddering sigh, almost like it had heard me.

Death's voice came out tired, his expression unreadable. "You'd better be ready, Grave Girl. Because this is only the beginning."

SIX

E vil Eye Burials always managed to get under my skin in a way Shepherd's Rest never did.

Maybe it was the statues. Normal cemeteries had leaning angels and weather-stained crosses, but Evil Eye had, well, *eyes*. Carved into marble, set into mosaics, even dangling from wrought-iron gates. Unblinking, wide, and glossy with magic, they always looked alive. Watching. Waiting. Judging.

Mist licked over the raised beds like swamp breath. The air was colder here, sharp enough to sting my nose. My blade vibrated against my spine, restless, like it could taste the layers of centuries pressed into the soil, and sense the random spirits that clung to the property.

"You'd think all cemeteries would feel the same," I muttered, pulling my jacket tighter as I crunched along a gravel path dotted with overgrown weeds. "Dead people, dead flowers, bad lighting." My voice came out thin, betraying how tightly wound I was. "But no. This one has to go for demonic Disney ride vibes."

Ghost's ears perked, tail a jaunty flag. She seemed immune to the place's oppressive air, but every few steps her head snapped toward a statue of a raven with its beak gaping, or a skeleton monument carved with its hands over its eyes. She growled low each time, a quiet, canine warning.

The earthbound spirits watched me, too, their eyes rheumy and vacant. A few were shades, others creations that Aurora had crafted to scare people away. Any time one came too close, the scythe vibrated harder, and my grim tattoo burned. They both wanted me to reap the spirits. Normally, I would, but that wasn't on my agenda tonight.

A crow cawed somewhere high in the yews, its voice hoarse and broken. The sound scraped along my nerves. "How Aurora lives here is beyond me," I whispered, more for myself than Ghost. "Witch or not, this place feels like it's already halfway to the Underworld. I can't even imagine waking up with these statues staring at me before I've had coffee."

Ghost sneezed in reply, which I chose to interpret as a sign of agreement.

I trudged after her, the mausoleum that housed Aurora's home rising ahead like something out of a gothic horror movie. Its columns were wrapped in ivy, its lintel etched with a row of eyes. The mist pooled heavily around its base, and I swear I heard a faint whispering that stopped the second I lifted my head to listen.

Two gargoyles peered down at me with leering grins, and if I didn't know better, I'd think they were sentient. They were probably the ones whispering.

I blew out a breath, fogging the air. I'd texted my friend to tell her I was coming, so I wasn't surprised when the heavy oak door creaked open. Andy stood framed in the threshold, a dark shape against the glow of witchlight behind him.

He looked rough. Not in the way of a man who'd just run five miles, but in the way of someone carrying a weight no workout could burn off. His shoulders were hunched, his jaw set, and he shoved his hands so deep in his pants pockets I wondered if he meant to keep them there forever.

"About time," he muttered. His eyes flicked over me and down to Ghost, who gave a wag. The movement cracked something in his face—not quite a smile, but close enough.

I stopped a few feet short, the damp air clinging to my face. "You know, most people greet guests with 'Welcome, can I get you a drink?' You? You're giving the brooding gargoyles a run for their money."

His jaw ticked with that faint smile again. "Just doing my part to fit in."

We trudged through the outer sanctum, going deep to Aurora's secret quarters. We passed several coffins before I glimpsed the familiar glow of her atrium-laboratory-library hybrid over his shoulder.

Inside, shelves rose like cathedral walls, candles flickered beside jars of herbs, and whatever she was brewing inside the bubbling cauldron hanging over the fire gave off the scent of rosemary and copper. No evil eyes, leering gargoyles, or shades in here.

The scythe went quiet, finally, and I unbuckled the holder as Ghost raced across to greet Aurora's cat. "Please tell me you're cooking dinner and not boiling frogs," I said to Andy.

The look he gave my blade wasn't envy so much as hunger. A reminder of what he'd lost—and what he'd never stop missing. He closed the door behind us, and the silence felt too heavy, as if the cemetery itself had been shut out and wasn't happy about it. "She'll be out in a minute."

It was warm and homey here, and I glanced at the waterfall trickling down one stone wall, its pool glowing faintly as if moonlight swam inside it.

After greeting the cat, who hissed and swatted at her nose, Ghost trotted straight to the hearth rug and circled a few times before flopping down.

Aurora appeared from behind one of her bookshelves. There was a smear of dust on her cheek and ink smudges on her fingers. "I've gathered all the grimoires and texts I could find that might shed light on things."

"Your cemetery hasn't gotten any less creepy," I told her, eyeing a particularly large plant whose leaves looked suspiciously like they wanted to reach out and shake my hand. "But in here, it's pure magic."

Aurora's mouth curved. "It's been a while since you visited."

Andy gravitated toward the hearth and crouched in

front of the flames like he needed their heat more than anyone else in the room. He petted Ghost, but his eyes tracked Aurora. When she glanced at him, his gaze skittered away.

I made myself comfortable on a stool at her worktable, which was strewn with herb cuttings, crystals, and an assortment of other witchy items. "Show me the books that might tell us how to deal with the Ferryman before I start stress-eating your potion herbs."

Aurora's cat hopped onto the table and flicked its tail from atop an open grimoire. Aurora shoved a small stack of books across the expanse, their spines cracked, leather faded, and with more bookmarks than a librarian's fever dream peeking out from between dozens of pages. "I've marked the most relevant passages," she said. "Most of these reference tide-takers, or entities who move between realms without sanction. There are fragments, too—poems, riddles. Not much detail, but enough to confirm he's real."

She laid one heavier tome aside, its cover bound in mottled brown hide, the clasp tarnished silver. "And this one has an ancient reference to the first reaper—you. I thought it might be relevant after what you told me."

That one called to me, but I wanted to save it until I understood more about my latest enemy. I tugged the top book toward me, flipping pages already softened to tissue. "Death says Oblivion is behind this. He's some big, bad entity who's older than gods, older than the Veil itself."

She quirked her head. "I think I've come across that name, but not recently."

"He called the Ferryman Oblivion's hand. It sounds like he's not ferrying souls anywhere at all, just feeding them into some cosmic disposal."

Aurora's eyes sharpened, emerald bright. She tapped her chin with one ink-smudged finger. "Oblivion. Of course. Wait here." She spun, her skirts flying out in the breeze she created, and headed for the far shelf with the brisk excitement of someone who knew exactly where to find a hidden cookie.

As she vanished, Andy wandered closer. He dragged one of the grimoires toward him and flipped it open, thumbing through the pages without really looking at them.

I leaned on an elbow, yawning, and kept my tone casual. "How are you holding up?"

"Fine." The word snapped like a mousetrap. He slammed the book shut, the sound making Ghost lift her head. His eyes were flat, and he turned on his heel and strode out of the room, boots echoing against the stone floor.

"Smooth," I muttered, guilt prickling.

Aurora returned, a different volume hugged to her chest. She stopped short, glancing toward the hall where Andy had disappeared. Her expression softened, lines of worry pulling at her mouth. "He's still struggling," she said quietly, setting the new book down. "I'm walking on eggshells around him."

I offered a sympathetic smile. "Is there anything I can do?"

Her fingers trailed over the cover distractedly. "He

doesn't know who he is without his magic. He was raised to be a wolf, to not only protect the pack, but to lead it. Now, he feels lost." She hesitated, then sighed. "I've been searching for a reversal—an elixir, a spell, anything that might counter Killion's dragon fire. Nothing so far. His dragon fire is ancient, alien. It burned out those bugs, but it also burned Andy's magic out at the root."

I thought of Killion's hands on mine last night, pouring healing through me after the scythe burned me. His fire could save and destroy in the same breath. "You're sure Andy's wolf is gone for good?"

Aurora's eyes were bleak. "It's awful, but I'm afraid so."

I wanted to say something encouraging, to throw her a lifeline of hope, but I honestly didn't know what it would be. I'd never encountered such a thing in my short time as a reaper, and although my magic hadn't been part of me for very long, I couldn't imagine life without it. My heart went out to Andy, and I made a mental note to start my own search for a remedy. If nothing else, there had to be a way to give him purpose again, magic or not.

We both dug into the books, me skimming the highlighted passages in the book I'd selected, while she made notes in a journal as she cross-referenced several grimoires.

Ghost's low growl made the hair on the back of my neck stand up. She left her comfy spot in front of the hearth to cross the floor, her hackles lifted. Her gaze was fixed on the upper shelves.

From across the way, my scythe hummed in its

holster, its power calling to me. I followed Ghost's stare—and for half a second, I could have sworn I saw pale, translucent fingers rifling the spines of the books.

The air shifted, sending a cool breeze past my cheek. Pages of the book in front of me fluttered.

Aurora barely glanced in that direction, whispered a few words under her breath, and sketched a sigil in the air with her fingers. The disturbance fizzled out like smoke in the rain. The book stilled. The air warmed again.

"Even the dead want answers," she said.

Andy reappeared in the doorway a few minutes later, shoulders tense, jaw working. He didn't quite meet my eyes at first. "Sorry about earlier," he muttered. "I shouldn't have snapped. I could have helped last night if I wasn't...broken. It's been eating me up."

Aurora's worry slipped into vexation. "You're not broken, Andy. You're alive."

I closed the book, watching him like I'd watch a dog I knew might bite but secretly just needed a hug. "We're all stretched thin." I tipped my chin toward the stack of grimoires. "Sit. Help me before I drown in ancient ink. And remember, alive is still on the winning team."

Something flickered across his face — doubt, maybe, but also relief. He dragged a stool over and dropped onto it, the wood creaking under his weight. He reached for one of the books.

Giving a mental sigh of my own relief, I exchanged a quick glance with Aurora. She dipped her chin in silent thanks. I flipped past dry passages about spectral bindings and archaic rites until Andy elbowed me.

"Here," he said. He angled his volume toward me.

The passage was written in faded script, ink brown with age. I read it out loud, *"The First was not forged as a weapon alone. It is a seam-keeper, wrought to stitch tears in the Veil. It remembers its bearer. If ever it refuses, the Veil itself may be undone."*

My chest tattoo pulsed, heat blooming beneath my skin. "So if my blade decides to ghost me, the whole world unravels. No pressure."

Aurora tapped her own book with the tip of her purple pen. "Listen to this." Her voice threaded through the bubbling of the cauldron. *"The Tide-Taker comes when balance falters, stealing souls before they reach their rightful ends. He does not ferry—he rends. He is tied to unmaking, a herald of Oblivion's reach."*

She paused, her gaze grave as she read the final line. *"Where the First scythe mends, the Ferryman rends."*

A chill rippled through me. I took both tomes and stared at the passages until they began to blur. "So it's me and my moody blade against Oblivion's personal oarsman."

Aurora's lips pressed into a thin line. "Chloe, if the First Blade really is the only thing keeping the Veil stitched, and it's already burning you..." Her gaze dropped to my hand, where the blisters from last night were gone, but their ghosts still remained. "That might mean it's starting to reject you. If Oblivion is unraveling your bond with it, then—"

"Then he can rip the Veil wide open," Andy finished, voice tight.

The silence that dropped between us was thick enough to choke on. Even the waterfall sounded muted. The cauldron stopped bubbling.

I pressed a hand to my chest where my grim tattoo felt like an ember under skin. "So if the scythe quits on me..." My voice came out quiet, ragged at the edges. "The Veil quits on everyone?"

Aurora didn't answer. She didn't have to.

"Well." I grabbed the books and stacked them to take with me. I wanted to show Killion what I'd found. "I guess the First and I better work out our issues fast." I peeked over at the blade, quiet now, as if it were listening closely. "If the Ferryman's already on his way, we don't have time to lose."

SEVEN

By the time I got back to the penthouse, I was wired. I dumped the stack of grimoires on the coffee table with a thunk that made Ghost's ears flick. She hopped onto the couch and curled up like she'd been the one schlepping ancient lore all night.

Killion emerged from his office, eyes skimming the pile of cracked spines and yellow sticky notes. "Some light bedtime reading or a documentary in the making?"

I dropped into the cushions beside Ghost, rubbing my face. "Aurora's library had everything except a how-to pamphlet titled Surviving Oblivion for Dummies. These are the highlights." He sank down on the cushion on my other side as I flipped one of the grimoires open, the faded ink making my eyes ache. "We found passages saying the First Blade doesn't just reap—it stitches the Veil. And if it refuses its bearer"—I pointed to my chest—"it can undo everything."

"Refuses?" His tone sharpened around the word. "You mean rejects you."

My burned palm pulsed at the reminder. I flexed it and closed the book harder than necessary. "Feels like it already has one foot out the door. And if that happens, we're all screwed."

Killion tugged me to him, easing us both back on the couch. In the glow coming from the fireplace, his features looked carved in stone. "Your scythe has moods. So do you. But it's bound to you—it remembers you. Whatever Oblivion thinks he can unravel, he'll fail."

I gave him a look. "What I can't understand is why Death didn't tell me all of this before now."

"Maybe he doesn't know."

I gave him an incredulous look. "How could he *not* know that if the First Blade rejects me, the entire universe could vanish?"

"Although he acts as though he is the smartest person in the room, he is not. Oblivion is something more ancient than any of us, which is exceptionally rare."

I tapped my fingers against my thigh. "You're right. I'm not sure I understand how Oblivion can be older than the gods, but whatever." I glanced at the scythe, hanging in its holder on a hook by the door. It had been completely quiet since I'd left Aurora's. "Surely, this isn't the first time my blade and I have encountered him, though."

"An all-powerful being is after my wife. I think I'm jealous."

I smacked his arm. "You make it sound like I want to

be the center of his attention. He wants to kill me, not flirt with me."

His mouth curved, just a little. "We actually aren't sure what he wants from you, outside of the weapon. This isn't the first time someone has tried to steal it from you for nefarious purposes."

Nefarious. Such a Killion word. A laugh slipped out before I could stop it. It felt good—normal—to find some levity in all of this. "I hate malevolent entities with nefarious intent."

He kissed my temple. "We must prepare for the worst, but we will prevail."

I leaned forward and kissed him, tasting warmth and certainty and everything opposite of the cold gnawing at my guts. When I pulled back, I whispered, "Don't make promises you can't keep."

"I never do." His gaze searched mine, steady. "You've overcome great obstacles before. You will again. I will be by your side through it all."

The next kiss turned deeper, hotter. It was half an hour before we came up for air. We sorted through the books, organizing them into piles, and finally dragged ourselves to bed. A part of me wanted to leave the scythe hanging by the door, but another wanted it close. I brought it to the bedroom and propped it next to the nightstand.

Ghost claimed the end of the mattress, and I let Killion tuck me against his chest, his arm heavy and grounding. The city hummed around us, and exhaustion pulled me under. But even in sleep, my grim tattoo burned—like it knew peace was on borrowed time. Sleep didn't stay peaceful.

I dreamed of water, endless and black, lapping at my boots. The sound of oars echoed across the void, *splash, splash, splash*—steady as a heartbeat. Fog thickened until I couldn't see my own hands. Then came the clink of chains, slow and deliberate, like someone dragging anchors across stone.

A figure rose from the mist, faceless, cloaked, and impossibly tall. His shadow bled into the horizon, swallowing it whole. He lifted something—my scythe—and the glow along its blade was crimson, not silver. It pulsed in time with my tattoo, searing so hot I cried out.

I bolted upright in bed, gasping. The scythe lay quiet against the nightstand, but my chest burned. Killion stirred, instantly alert, his hand warm on my arm. "Chloe?"

Before I could answer, my phone buzzed. The screen lit up with a name that made me frown—Andy.

I swiped it open, still breathing hard. "What's wrong? Are you okay? Is Aurora?"

"She's fine." His voice was tight, words clipped. "You need to meet me. Now."

Cold sweat slicked the back of my neck. "Where?"

"The safe house." He hesitated, like the words were costing him. "There's something you have to see."

Killion sat up fully, the tension in his body mirroring mine. I caught the faint violet shimmer in his eyes. He didn't ask what Andy wanted—he'd heard the whole thing.

"Give me five minutes," I told Andy.

"Hurry." His voice was impatient. "Bring the scythe. You'll understand when you get here." And then he hung up.

Killion's hand closed around mine. "If he's calling before dawn, it isn't nothing."

"No kidding." I swung out of bed, grabbing for my jeans. Ghost leapt down from the mattress, tail stiff, ears pinned, already in alert mode.

Killion pulled on his shirt, eyes locked on me. "We go together."

"Always," I said, strapping the blade to my back.

By the time we pulled into the driveway, dawn was only a faint rumor on the horizon. The safe house loomed against the thinning mist, exactly as it had been the last time I'd been here—tall, narrow, and perpetually on the verge of collapse.

The concrete steps had chunks missing like teeth knocked out in a bar fight. The porch sagged under the weight of a couple of battered chairs, a rickety table, and a graveyard of whiskey bottles. And because apparently no one here believed in seasonal storage, the plastic Christmas tree still stood sentinel in one corner, half its colored lights burned out, the star topper slouching as if it was giving up on life.

A metal plaque with the wolf pack insignia hung over the door, tarnished but still gleaming in the dim light.

I climbed the steps, Ghost ahead of me, sniffing at the air with wary determination. Killion was a quiet shadow at my side, scanning the yard, the trees beyond, the road we'd just come from. His tension only made mine worse.

Andy opened the door before I could knock. His hair was mussed, his shoulders hunched like the weight he carried had only grown since I saw him a few hours ago. "You came." Relief flickered across his face, but it was quickly swallowed by something grimmer. He glanced at Killion, then at the scythe strapped across my back. "Come on."

The inside smelled of stale smoke, old wood, and the faint iron tang of shifter magic. Also, wet dog. The walls bore claw marks I chose not to ask about.

Andy led us down a narrow hall into a back room, where the curtains had been drawn tight. A lamp glowed over a battered table, and sitting at it was a boy, maybe nine or ten, with a shock of red hair and eyes fixed on the paper in front of him. His hands moved fast, sketching with a stubby pencil like the world might unravel if he stopped.

Andy stood behind the boy's chair. "This is Caleb. I asked his parents to give us a few minutes with him."

The table was already covered in dozens of drawings. Some were even scattered across the floor. At first glance, they looked like the usual monsters a kid might imagine, but my stomach dropped when I recognized the long oars, cloaked figure, and shadowed river.

The Ferryman.

Each drawing showed him in a different scene— reaching from the mist, dragging chains, leaning over a crowd of faceless souls. Mountains of coins at his feet.

The more I looked, the more I realized they weren't random sketches. They seem to tell a story.

Ghost whined low and pressed against my leg. Killion studied them closely. *What do you make of it*, he asked telepathically through our bond.

I shook my head. "Caleb, these are incredible," I said. "You're exceptionally talented."

The boy didn't look up. Didn't even blink. His pencil scraped over the paper, frantic, relentless. He hummed.

Andy's voice was rough, quiet. "He doesn't talk much. But he doesn't have to." He gestured at the drawings. "This is what he sees. He's been diagnosed with autism. His parents think his drawings are just his imagination, as disturbing as they are. I know better."

My throat felt tight as I crouched beside the table, eyes sweeping over the latest page. The Ferryman was there again, cloaked and faceless—but this time he held something unmistakable.

My scythe. In the next sketch, he raised it high, angled toward a figure on her knees. I couldn't see the victim's face, but I knew those boots.

I stood and looked down. Yep, they were the same as my boots.

My stomach turned to ice. The only thing I could hear was the thrum of my pulse, a steady drumbeat of dread, and the boy's pencil on the paper.

He scribbled harder, adding streaks of black around the Ferryman's hood, darker and darker until the paper nearly tore. His hum rose in pitch. Ghost whined again, but now pressed against *his* leg, like she was trying to anchor him in the storm of whatever he saw.

Andy swore under his breath. Killion's hand brushed mine.

I dragged my gaze from the drawing, throat tight. "He's not just imagining monsters," I said hoarsely. "He's seeing what's coming."

Killion's fingers tightened around mine, his grip steady but his eyes sharp with calculation. "It's a story, a prophecy."

Andy's jaw flexed, his whole body tensing. "That's what I think, too."

Caleb's pencil slowed, his humming dropping to a low drone. He glanced sideways at Ghost, and his small hand found the dog's fur for just a heartbeat before he went back to shading the Ferryman's cloak.

The room felt too small, the air too thin. I pressed my palm to my grim tattoo, throbbing in time with my heartbeat. Heat pulsed out of it, answering the blade on my back. The Ferryman. My scythe. *Me on my knees.*

I swallowed hard. "We need every one of these drawings. All of them so that we can lay them out in order."

Andy's brows drew together. "You really think they're a prophecy?"

"I think," I said, forcing my voice to steady, "that Caleb just handed us the closest thing to a playbook we're going to get. And if we're smart, we can rewrite the ending before it gets that far."

EIGHT

The former Catholic church loomed over this corner of Dante's Grove with old stone and cracked stained glass. Its spire sat slightly crooked these days, as though it was trying to lean away from the rest of the town.

Our Blessed Mother sat near the front steps, also leaning, and looked on with a hollow sadness that made her seem hopeless. Colored beaded necklaces were layered around her neck, their cheap, gaudy appearance in contrast to her dirty blue and white robes.

Killion had bought the place decades ago and, through his magic, kept it human-free now. The wards that hung over it repelled anyone he wanted to look the other way, and though the parishioners were long gone, the smell of incense still clung faintly to the air inside, much like the heavy layer of guilt all strict Catholics seemed to embrace.

We filed inside—me, Killion, Andy, and Ghost, with

the stack of Caleb's drawings wrapped tight under my arm. The wooden doors groaned shut behind us, muting the early morning traffic coming from outside.

Shadows lingered thick in the pews, the only light the fractured reds and blues that bled through stained glass windows depicting saints whose eyes looked a little too accusatory for my taste.

Mary's mother, St. Anne, stood tall and regal by the dais, her tall, stone figure staring down on us with mild disdain.

"Remind me why vampires always get the creepiest real estate," I muttered.

"Tradition," Killion said, like it was obvious. His designer shoes echoed softly off the flagstones as he led the way past the transept. "And intimidation. Both are effective."

Ghost padded along at my heels, her nose twitching at the smell of damp stone and lingering blood that no amount of scrubbing would ever completely erase.

Katarina emerged from a side chamber, all leather and precision. She moved like a blade made human, and her once black-as-night hair was bleached to platinum blond. She'd pulled it back into a severe knot, but still had her bangs. "Master," she said, inclining her head to Killion. Then her gaze swept over me and Andy with an expression that matched Anne's. "And guests."

I lifted the bundle of drawings. "How good are you at puzzles?"

Before she could answer, the side door banged open, and Aurora hustled in. "Andy texted," she said, cheeks pink from the cold. Her eyes found him, and for a heart-beat, the lines of strain around her mouth softened. "How did you know Caleb had this gift?"

Andy's shoulders went back an inch, pride lacing his posture. His jaw unclenched, and there wasn't bitterness in his voice as he spoke. "I did the intake on him and his parents so they could stay at the safe house until we found passage for them to the Northern Wilds. There's a camp up there for supernatural kids. They'll help Caleb manage his gifts, including his ability to shift when the time comes. As soon as I saw his drawings, I knew there was a reason they ended up here right now."

That pleased look in his eyes did more for me than the heat of the church's ancient furnace. For the first time in days, he looked like Andy again—not just the hollowed-out version grief and loss had left behind.

Aurora caught my gaze and smiled faintly, as if she noticed the change, too. "I'm so glad you and the pack are here for them. It must be horribly difficult to raise a gifted child like that in the no-mag world."

No-mag was a term for humans with no magic.

We carried everything to the wide oak table that had once held the chalice and bread of communion, but now bore the scuffs and knife marks of vampire training. I spread Caleb's drawings across it, weighing down the curling edges with brass candleholders. The kid's frantic pencil strokes came alive under the fractured light, the Ferryman's faceless figure looming again and again.

Killion stood beside me, hands clasped behind his

back, his expression carved from stone. Andy and Aurora leaned over opposite sides, their faces drawn tight.

"It's a progression," Aurora murmured. "A narrative."

I nodded. "Yeah. The problem is, the scenery in some of them is vague." I touched a sketch where the Ferryman loomed against jagged lines. "This could be mountains, or the edge of the city. Or just abstract scribbles. Hard to tell."

Katarina crossed her arms, unimpressed by prophecy or pencil. "I know this town better than anyone." She pointed to a succession of images. "That's Shepherd's Rest, that's the old lumber sawmill."

I tapped one of the drawings that brought back nightmares. "And that's the catacombs where the vamps tried to kill Andy and me."

He met my eyes with a solemn nod. It had been a year since the rogue vampires had caused so much trouble, but neither of us would forget what they'd done to us. "I recognize it, too."

"But these"—I poked at several more like the one dominated by the Ferryman and not much else—"are too nebulous. I can't build a solid timeline for the story unless I know where they fit in."

Katarina leaned forward to study the one my finger was still on. "There's a monument or something to the left of the hooded creep. It's not much to go off of, but we can look for it." She waved a hand over the table. "I'll make copies of these, and each of us can take a set. We split up and canvas the town, cross-referencing the drawings with the landmarks."

"Like a scavenger hunt," Aurora said.

"As long as this hunt doesn't end with me dead," I uttered.

The shadows in the church bent unnaturally. Cold slid over my skin, a tide rolling in where no tide should exist.

Ghost yipped and wagged her tail. Then the air split, and Death stepped out of the seam between light and shadow, a long coat whispering around him like it had been stitched from midnight.

His eyes roamed over the table of drawings, pausing long enough to make the hair rise on my arms. "You didn't invite me to your crayons and cartoons club?"

"The invite must have gotten lost in the mail," I said, a bit wearily. While the vampire blood in me kept me from needing as much sleep as I had previously, I was still running a few hours—entire nights—too low. "These are sketches by a young shifter boy that Andy knows. Caleb appears to be seeing the Ferryman before he arrives. These pictures,"—I shoved one of the papers toward him, Ferryman looming, scythe raised—"are glimpses of what's coming."

Death tilted his head, his expression unreadable. "So the child dreams. That doesn't make him an oracle."

Andy bristled. "He's not dreaming, and it's not his imagination. He *is* an oracle."

Killion studied the drawing of me on my knees and my scythe in the hands of the Ferryman. "This is what we're facing. The boy has offered us a timeline of what's to come. We'd be foolish not to use this tool to stop the Veil from falling."

Andy moved to Killion's side, the three of us now forming a wall. "He's seeing the future and showing us where the Ferryman will be next," I said. "All we need to do is be prepared."

"We can trap the Ferryman," Killion added, ever the strategist. He rubbed his chin, his violet eyes filled with the promise of death to him if he so much as touched me. "The battle will be over before it can begin."

Death's gaze slid to Andy, then the pictures, and I swore the room dropped a few degrees. "Interesting that a magicless boy sees the clearest."

Andy flinched. "He's not a no-mag. He's a fox shifter, and believe it or not, they have a wide range of incredible powers."

Killion didn't move, but his magic was enough to alter the current in the room. He spoke to Death in a low and measured voice. "We don't dismiss evidence because it doesn't fit your preferred narrative."

For a breath, the two of them locked eyes—and invisible horns. The immovable force versus the immovable shadow. Then Death turned back to the table, studying the drawings more closely. His mouth thinned. "It seems Oblivion enjoys leaving breadcrumbs."

"Breadcrumbs that end with me on my knees about to be impaled by my own blade," I muttered.

Katarina snorted. "I'll have these mapped to the grid by sundown. If the Ferryman likes breadcrumbs, let's see if we can predict where he drops the next one."

Death's eyes flicked to me, sharp as a knife's edge. "I believe the Ferryman used the vampire and the tether to the witch to break through. You said she sent sparks of magic at you and a few hit the blade, right?"

I nodded.

"That's why it's been rejecting you. Her magic, mixed with the Ferryman's power, short-circuited something. You have to figure out how to reset it. If we keep the Veil intact, Oblivion won't stand a chance."

"We need to be prepared in case we can't manage that," Killion said. "We need a plan, and we lay a trap as a backup in case he makes it through."

Aurora rubbed a crystal between her fingers. "He needs water."

"Water sometimes flows in the catacombs." Killion placed a hand on my lower back, flooding my body with his magic as he sent a jolt of energy through the bond. He could feel I was flagging.

"They were flooded long ago," Katarina added. "Forgotten by most folks around here."

I raised a hand weakly. "Not excited about revisiting them."

Andy had paled. "Same."

I brushed the back of his hand with mine and lowered my voice. "You don't need to be part of this."

"I *am* part of this," he growled.

I knew he wasn't angry per se, that I'd simply touched a nerve. I squeezed his hand. "And I'm glad you're here."

That flustered him, and he shuffled his feet, but he

gave me a brief squeeze back before finding a pew to collapse on.

Aurora glanced at him, then locked eyes with me. "That could be the place he gathers strength before surfacing, circumventing the Veil altogether."

Killion's power sat up straighter at that idea. "The ripple in Shepherd's Rest could be nothing more than a distraction." He glared at Death. "We need a plan B *and* C."

Katarina checked the belt of weapons slung around her waist. "What does it take to kill him? Bullets? Steel?"

"You're thinking of him all wrong." Death paced in a circle around us and the table. "Killing him outright isn't like staking a vampire or banishing a demon—it's like trying to erase a shadow when the person casting it is still standing there. He's Oblivion's hand. He's not fully independent, more like a fragment or extension of something older, darker, and hungrier."

Killion leaned on the table, wave after wave of his power flowing through me. "If he's an extension, he can be severed."

"By my blade?" I asked, hopefully.

Death rounded the edge near Katarina and gave a nod. "There's a polarity between him and your scythe."

"*Where the First mends,*" Aurora said softly, "*the Ferryman rends.*"

Death's heavy footsteps echoed in my ears as he passed behind me. "He *can* be banished back into Oblivion's void and sealed there." He stopped, eyeing one of the pictures that showed The Ferryman at Shepherd's

Rest. "Your blade is literally the only thing that can 'cut' him back into nothingness and repair the Veil to keep him and Oblivion out of this world."

But Oblivion was unraveling my bond to the scythe. I pulled it from its holder and examined it. It was quiet, not thrumming or speaking. It felt almost...inert. Lifeless. "What if the blade rejects me when it's time to confront The Ferryman?"

Everyone's attention landed on the weapon. Death sighed. "You'll need to reassert your bond with it to make sure that doesn't happen."

"How?" Andy asked from his pew.

Death turned away from all of us, studying St. Anne as if the answer lay with the statue. "It will require...a sacrifice."

I didn't like the sound of that.

Killion bristled, a protective hand landing on me again. "What kind?"

Death waved him off. "It won't come to that. For now, we focus on repairing the Veil and keeping him out."

"You and Chloe go to the cemetery," Katarina said. "Killion and I will take the catacombs."

Death quirked a brow at the vampire, as if reminding her he didn't take orders from anyone.

Aurora tossed her crystal into her bag and started gathering the pictures. "What about me?"

Andy shot to his feet. "And me?"

Death ignored both of them, heading for the exit with a gesture for me to follow. "Chloe, bring the blade."

I folded my arms, pulse ticking hard in my throat. "No."

That got their attention. Even Katarina blinked. Death stopped, his voice slicing the silence. "Excuse me?"

I locked my knees and shoved the scythe back in its holder. "I have work in an hour. It's surgery day at the clinic—six patients on the docket. Killion and Katarina can check the catacombs, and Aurora and Andy can keep tabs on the cemetery. I'll contact Diego and fill him in on what's happening." Die was another reaper and my protege. I'd worked with him quite a bit through the summer, and he was doing better. He needed to be in on all of our plans. "Killion can send a group of his nest out with copies of the pictures to match them up with land-marks. We regroup at sundown and make a solid plan A." I glanced at Killion, who was trying to hide a smirk at my wresting control away from Death. "And a couple of backup plans, too."

Aurora's mouth opened, then closed. Andy gawked at me.

Death's voice dropped. "You would put mongrels and parakeets before the unraveling of the Veil?"

"Don't call them that," I shot back, angry. "They're my patients. They're living beings. They and their owners trust me to keep them safe and cared for. If I walk away now, I'm no better than Oblivion ripping souls out of the world." Death was all about keeping the universal balance—I was just trying to maintain some semblance of *life* balance. "Balance doesn't only mean fighting monsters—it means honoring life."

Death's mouth curved—not into a smile, but into something sharper. "You're about to end up dead, and that's what you're worried about?"

Killion slid an arm around my waist. "I'll take her to the clinic after we stop for coffee." His voice deepened, steady as iron. "You and the others can begin your hunt. Katarina will make the copies and round up a team to begin searching for the landmarks. After I deliver Chloe to work, I'll head to the catacombs."

The tension crackled like lightning between them— Death's shadow, Killion's flame, my stubborn heartbeat pounding between.

For once, Death looked away first. His jaw clenched, his hands flexing at his sides. "So be it. Play veterinarian while the world ends. But remember—when the Ferryman reaches for you, he won't wait for convenient scheduling."

He vanished, and everyone exhaled.

I leaned into Killion's steadiness. "Thank you," I whispered, low enough for only him.

His hand pressed at the small of my back. "Always."

NINE

The Smoking Bean smelled like sugar, caffeine, and heaven to my caffeine addiction.

Warm cinnamon and espresso steam wrapped around me the second I stepped inside, chasing off the damp chill that clung to Danté's Grove mornings. The familiar hiss of milk frothing, the clink of mugs, and the low hum of music under soft chatter—it all hit me in the chest with memories.

"Look who crawled out of the cemetery," Mason called from behind the counter, his grin pure mischief. His hair, dyed a defiant violet today, peeked from under his beanie, and his barista apron hung crooked. The violet matched Killion's eyes, and I figured that was intentional. Killion was like a father to him.

"Morning, trouble," I said, leaning against the counter. "How's my girl Ambrosia? Still purring?"

He patted the gleaming espresso machine with exaggerated affection. "She misses you something fierce, Doc.

She sulks whenever I use almond milk instead of whole. It's tragic."

"You need to whisper sweet nothings to her and sing the song of her people if she doesn't cooperate. Also, sometimes a sharp whack on her right side will get her to cough up the goods."

He laughed, flashing the faint hint of fang that only I'd catch if I looked closely. The vamp glamour hid everything else from the human customers. "Don't worry, I treat her like royalty. Even descaled her last night. She shines for me now."

I rolled my eyes, though warmth tugged at my lips. "Show-off."

The exhaustion under my skin prickled, an ache that caffeine couldn't cure, but nostalgia helped. The Bean had been my last regular job before grim work interfered. Early mornings were filled with caramel drizzle and gossip, not ghosts and graveyards.

Killion walked in, and every human head in the café turned toward him, as they always did, drawn by something they couldn't name—too handsome, too perfect, too *other*. His tailored coat brushed his knees as he crossed to me, radiating an authority that didn't belong in a place with tip jars and mismatched mugs.

Mason's smirk widened. "Hey, Master. You want the usual?"

"Espresso, triple shot, to hide the bitterness of existence," Killion said dryly. He glanced at me. "And for her, syrup pretending to pass as caffeine."

I raised a brow. "Mock my coffee and see if you get a kiss later."

Mason choked on a laugh. "You two are quite the couple."

"Love builds character." Killion slid a card across the counter as I eyed the muffins, cookies, and scones. I motioned to three items for Mason to bag for my breakfast. "And cavities, apparently."

Mason took the payment, still grinning, and winked at me. "Don't worry, Ambrosia and I will make your usual just the way you like it—extra whip, enough caramel to coat your soul. It will go perfectly with the brown sugar scone."

"You spoil me." I leaned on the counter, watching him work, my heart tugged by something simple and sweet. This place, including Mason, was still part of me.

Killion brushed my arm lightly, his voice low. "You miss it."

"Sometimes," I admitted while Mason built our drinks. "Back when my biggest problem was running out of oat milk."

He smiled faintly. "You'd be bored within a week now."

"Probably," I said, but I wasn't sure I believed it.

Mason slid a steaming cup and lid across to me before he grabbed another paper cup to pour Killion's coffee. "There you go, Mistress. Don't say I never make you anything pretty."

I hated when the vampires called me that, but it was out of deference to Killion as much as it was to me. The caramel was drizzled in a perfect spiral. I took the cup, breathing in the sweet, burnt-sugar scent, and smiled. "You're the best, kid."

Mason leaned close, lowering his voice in a mock whisper. "Don't tell Killion. He's sensitive and jealous."

"I heard that," Killion said, but his mouth curved, eyes softening.

I felt a small piece of my world click back into place—warm, human, and fragile enough to make me ache.

The door jingled, and a gust of cool morning air swirled in, accompanied by leaves and my best friend, Nita.

My *human* best friend, who knew nothing about my side gig as Death's reaper. I'd kept it that way on purpose. She, my aunt and uncle, and most of my clinic employees thought I was just like them. They had no idea that magic and the supernatural existed.

She bustled in like a force of nature wrapped in scrubs. Her hoodie was unzipped halfway, revealing the clinic logo across her chest, and her hair—usually streaked a rich purple—was a fiery blend of russet and gold today. It set off her tan skin and dark eyes to perfection. She looked like autumn personified, pumpkin earrings dangling from her lobes.

"Morticia," she said, as she swept in for a hug. It was a nickname she'd given me during my night job at the morgue when I worked for my Uncle Morty. Another of my jobs that had paid the college bills and that I'd had to give up when I became a reaper. "You look like a raccoon who lost a fight with a coffee bean grinder."

I wasn't sure exactly what that meant, but I got the drift. "Morning to you, too, Gomez." I hugged her back, trying to ignore the way my arms felt like wet noodles. I glanced at her shirt. "Are you scheduled today?"

"A little birdy"—her gaze flicked to Killion and back —"told me you might need a stand-in." She stepped back, studying me with that sharp clinician's eye that could find a flea under armor. Her gaze dropped to the dark smudges under my eyes. "When's the last time you slept?"

Here we go. My mother was gone, but Nita did a fine job of imitating her. "Define sleep."

"Uh-huh." She folded her arms. "Don't you dare tell me you're heading to the clinic."

"We've got six patients lined up this morning. JR and O'Leary need me."

Her lips twitched. "And I passed my boards, remember?" She pointed her thumb at herself, pride softening her voice. "I scheduled myself to handle the two spay jobs. They'll handle the rest. You, my dear zombie vet, are going home."

I blinked. "Excuse me?"

She leaned in, lowering her voice but not her authority. "You're exhausted, Chloe. I can see it from space. You walk into that OR with your hands shaking, and one wrong move could cost a patient their life. Patients first, right? Isn't that what you're always drilling into our heads? If you're not steady, you're putting all of us at risk."

Her chastising was a slap—and a wake-up call—because whether I liked it or not, she was right.

My throat tightened. I'd told myself that I could overcome my exhaustion with this pit stop, but I'd been fighting ghosts, nightmares, and the end of the world for two days straight.

Killion sipped his espresso and said mildly, "I concur."

I shot him a glare. "You're not helping."

"On the contrary," he said, "I'm delighted someone else is brave enough to tell you to rest."

"You hear that?" Nita pointed at him, as if deputizing him. "You're on watch. Make sure she doesn't so much as touch a scalpel today."

I groaned, pinching the bridge of my nose. "I can still assist. They'll need help managing post-op, anesthesia—"

"You can *assist*," she cut in, "by not passing out on top of an open abdomen."

My stomach twisted with a mix of guilt and resignation. Damn her for being right. Again.

Nita softened her voice. "You're amazing at what you do, Chloe. But even superheroes need to recharge. The clinic will survive a day without you."

I sighed, staring down into the caramel spiral of my latte. "Fine. But I'm still going in to make sure everyone's prepped and stable."

She knew when to budge, if only a little. "And then you go home. I mean it."

"Bossy," I muttered.

"Competent," she corrected, accepting her usual

order from Mason, who'd gotten it ready while we'd been talking. "See you there."

She waved to Mason and Killion as she left, the sunlight catching the gold in her hair when she hit the sidewalk. The shop felt quieter but also lighter from her visit.

Killion leaned close, his mouth ghosting my temple. "You have good friends."

"Yeah," I murmured. "Which makes them really annoying."

The bell over the door jingled again, and the faint smell of ozone, grave dirt, and something that might've been powdered sugar announced Diego before he even made it to the counter.

He was wearing his shirt inside out, and there was a dark smear up his sleeve that could've been blood, mud, or grease. With him, it was anyone's guess.

"Morning, sinners," he called cheerfully. "Who's in charge of caffeine miracles? I've got souls to sort and not enough brain cells to do it without help."

Mason snorted behind the counter and started pulling shots. "You're gonna have to specify—coffee or confession?"

"Both," Diego said. "Double the espresso, half the guilt."

He spotted me and waved, then pointed at a cookie in the case. "Don't start without me, Frost. Saving the Veil's important and all, but I refuse to do it until after I have breakfast."

I cringed, hoping the humans who were staring at

him just thought he was drunk. Of course, in this town during October, discussions about ghosts, graveyards, and souls were not strictly out of the norm.

Before Diego could engage half the café in a discourse on existential crisis, Killion and I cornered him at a table near the back. Killion threw up a ward to mute our conversation.

Die flopped into a chair, slouching as he spoke around a mouthful of cookie. "So, why do I have the honor of meeting you at the crack of dawn in the land of pumpkin spice?"

Killion's expression didn't shift. "The Ferryman is real and trying to come through the Veil."

Leave it to my husband to get right to business. Diego's grin faded. "Is that good or bad?"

"You don't know who the Ferryman is?" I asked.

He shook his head, cookie crumbs falling from his chin to his shirt. "Should I?"

He wasn't like us. Not human, either. He'd been created in an otherworldly test tube of sorts by someone inside Soul Management Group who wanted to create souls. A big no-no. The culprit—or culprits—were still at large, but Die had ended up being enlisted by SMG into the ranks of reapers. He still had a great deal to learn about this world.

Killion and I exchanged a glance. I took a minute to fill in my grim protege, watching as his face fell.

Die blinked, reached for his cookie, which already gone, and then raised bewildered eyes to me. "We have to stop him?"

I nodded. "He's working for an entity called Obliv-ion. He's the bigger problem, but the Ferryman is the one we have to start with."

Diego rubbed a hand over his face. "So we're fighting, what, Oblivion's evil Uber driver?"

That was one way of putting it. "Only this one wants to drag all of us into the void for his master." I glanced at Killion. "And he most likely finds vampires to be the easiest targets because they walk the line between life and death."

Diego blinked. "No tip for that ride, then."

Despite myself, I snorted. Killion didn't, but his mouth twitched—his equivalent of a belly laugh.

I pulled one of Caleb's sketches from my bag, laying it flat on the table between us. The Ferryman's faceless shape loomed over the page like it was about to step out of it. "A gifted kid drew this and a dozen more like it. Caleb's a fox shifter, maybe ten. He's been sketching what's coming—visions of the Ferryman, the rifts, everything."

Die studied it, his easy humor dimming into some-thing more focused. "That's...so cool. Creepy, but look at the details. You sure Caleb's not channeling Death's Pinterest board?"

I shot him a look. "Diego."

He raised his hands. "Okay, okay. Serious face. You're saying this kid's seeing the future?"

"Yes," Killion said. "And it's a future we'd prefer to avoid. We're splitting up to locate the sites he's drawn—catacombs, cemeteries, old ruins. Because we aren't sure about all the locations, we're working in teams to identify them."

Diego slammed down his drink. "And I'm guessing this is the part where you tell me I get to help hunt a myth that's not a myth while trying not to die horribly."

I crossed my arms. "If you don't help and Oblivion succeeds, you're going to die a horrible death anyway."

"You constantly insist you want to be a part of Chloe's..." Killion paused. "Scooby gang. This is an opportunity for you to do exactly that."

"Right." Die nodded solemnly, dusting the crumbs from his shirt. "I was picturing more team-building exercises and fewer eldritch horrors, but sure. I'm in."

Killion's violet eyes glinted with something approving. "Good. You'll come with me to the catacombs."

Die blinked, then smiled weakly. "Fantastic. I've done all the ghost tours. Why not take the city's dampest hellhole tour?"

"We'll drop Chloe at the clinic and meet one of my nest at the site," Killion said, standing. "You'll be fine."

I wasn't so sure he would. Diego was brave, yes. Loyal, definitely. But the Ferryman wasn't just another monster in the dark.

As we gathered our things, Diego gave me a crooked grin. "Don't worry, boss. We'll handle the crypt crawl while you play Dr. Doolittle. Try not to get haunted by anything weird."

I raised a brow. "Have you met me?"

He laughed, bumping my arm lightly. "Fair. Guess we're all doomed, huh?"

"Probably," I said. "But we're doomed together."

Killion handed me what was left of my latte. "As encouraging as ever, darling."

I finished it off, letting the caramel and caffeine hit my bloodstream. I gave them a wink. "Hey, I'm an optimist. We'll all make it to lunchtime at least."

TEN

By midmorning, the overhead lights buzzed faintly, and the steady rhythm of clinking surgical instruments and murmured conversations was a lullaby to my overtired brain.

I was cataloging sutures when something cold brushed my ankle. I looked down and froze.

A translucent yellow tabby sauntered past my feet, tail flicking. She hopped up on the counter and strolled right through a tray of instruments. Her ghostly fur shimmered in the surgical light, and her paws left tiny frost prints on the metal.

"Hey there," I murmured under my breath, automatically shifting to block Nita's line of sight. Pointless, since Nita wasn't supernatural and didn't see ghosts. My friend was talking softly to our anesthesiologist, Clara, near the monitor, both of them oblivious. "You're not on today's schedule."

The cat stretched, yawned, and walked straight through a stack of towels.

Nita suddenly appeared beside me. "You good?"

"Yep," I said too brightly. "Just talking to myself."

She smirked. "Which confirms you need to go home and sleep."

The ghost cat jumped off the counter and flicked its tail at me before fading out of sight.

I exhaled slowly, counting to three, like that would make the goosebumps go away. No luck. The Veil had been humming all morning, a low vibration in my bones. I'd hoped it was leftover adrenaline from last night. It wasn't.

"Just a few more things to restock," I said.

JR entered, scrubbed and ready to tackle one of the spay clients. Nita and Clara went into action.

I'd barely turned back to the shelves when a flash of green zipped past my head. I ducked.

Two translucent parakeets swooped over the surgical lamps, wings scattering sparks of pale light. They chattered at each other in high-pitched ghost-bird nonsense.

"Not funny," I hissed under my breath. "This is a no-fly zone."

Ghost appeared in the doorway, eyes tracking the birds as they vanished through the ceiling.

My head throbbed, the Veil pressing at the edges of my skull. How could I go home and sleep with all of this going on?

Then came a fox kit, trotting past my boots in a shimmer of silver fur, followed by a hound with mournful eyes that made my grim tattoo flare hot beneath my scrubs.

I swallowed hard and hurriedly filled the gauze bin. "Okay," I whispered to the empty air. "Not good."

Ghost whined softly. I gestured her out of the OR and crouched to stroke her head in the hall. "If this keeps up," I muttered, "we'll need a whole new wing for ghost patients."

She huffed, ears twitching.

Sylvie stopped me for paperwork, and I signed off, promising I'd be heading home soon. I meant it, too. The clinic was stable, outside of the ghost animals, and JR and Nita had things handled. For once, the mortal world didn't need me.

I texted Killion's driver, Moss, to pick me up.

Outside, thunder rolled—a sound that had no business existing under clear blue skies. I checked my weather app, but no rain was predicted.

I was in the back room, checking post-op vitals, when my skin prickled—the telltale heat that always meant *him*.

Killion entered, violet eyes catching the overhead light. The lights flickered, once, twice. Then steadied again—brighter than before, too bright.

Every animal in the recovery ward froze.

"You sure know how to make an entrance," I said, though unease prickled up my spine.

His eyes darkened, and he smiled—a rare sight. "I thought you were simply glad to see me."

"I am." Certain body parts were extremely glad, in

fact, and wanted to jump his bones as soon as I got him alone. "But I'm not the one who caused that."

The grin vanished. His gaze went past me. Ghost growled.

"What is it?" I turned—and the temperature plummeted.

I saw nothing and was about to ask Killion what he sensed when Nita appeared in the doorway. "Did we just have a power surge?"

Sounded plausible. "Maybe," I lied. The air had gone cold enough to frost my breath.

Killion brushed past me, heading for the supply closet. "I'll check the breaker."

Ghost followed after him.

The clinic had gone silent. No barking or other animal noises, no clatter from the surgery room. The quiet was too complete, a vacuum sucking the sound right out of the world. I waved Nita off. "Don't worry. We'll handle it."

She left. I grabbed my bag, freeing my scythe, and squeezed into the supply closet. An out-of-place odor— stagnant water and metal—hit me full in the face.

A familiar shape coalesced in front of a crate stacked with bags of dog food, pulling itself together from smoke and darkness.

The scythe bucked in my hand. "Impossible," I breathed.

The vampire shade stepped forward, grinning with a mouth full of cracked fangs. His eyes were pits of dull silver, and liquid metal dripped from his fingertips, hissing where it hit the tile.

"You exploded," I said, shaking under my skin. I hated dead things that didn't have the decency to stay dead. "And you're not on my patient list."

Killion moved beside me. "Who are you?"

"Oblivion eats," the shade rasped, ignoring his question. The voice was dry, scraping, sandpaper on the walls. "It chews souls and spits out what it doesn't need."

The scythe vibrated hard. I wasn't sure I understood what that meant. "I'm confused. So Oblivion didn't need you?"

Coins rained from his hands, pinging off the floor with dull, metallic chimes. "I am the Ferryman's courier."

"Still not getting why you're here." I gripped the scythe handle tighter, smacking the blade in my other hand. "You shouldn't exist."

He laughed, a sound like breaking glass. "You can't reap what's already been eaten."

"Sounds...gross." My grim tattoo blazed hot under my scrubs. The air warped between us, rippling like heat over asphalt, only this wasn't heat. This was the Veil twisting. "Why are you here?"

He stepped closer, bare feet leaving streaks of metal that smoldered and vanished. "I come with a message. The tide's rising. The Ferryman's coming. You'll feel the pull soon."

Killion's magic flared into a protective bubble around us. Ghost bristled, her growl deep enough to vibrate the walls.

"You don't belong here," Killion said.

The shade's grin widened, but his focus never left me. "No one can save you, Reaper. The Ferryman always gets what Oblivion wants."

"You're quite scary," I said with deadly calm. A demeanor I'd learned from the master vampire. "This whole doomsday cryptic warning is cute, if a little over the top. Go back to the Veil and tell the Ferryman he'd better stick to his own river. This world is mine. He's not welcome here."

The overhead light flared and burst, showering us with sparks. I flinched, but Killion's bubble kept them from reaching me.

Coins spilled from the shade's mouth now. His eyes burned darker, silver turning to black. Somewhere beyond the Veil, something laughed—a deep, echoing sound that wasn't human.

The Ferryman? Oblivion?

The scythe burned my palm. I gasped—then the shade imploded, sucked backward into nothingness, leaving the smell of wet coins and that fading laughter.

Killion dropped the barrier. The silence roared in its wake.

Nita burst in, stopping short. "What just happened?" Her gaze dropped to my weapon. "Why do you have popcorn?"

The scythe shimmered, but all she saw was her favorite food. "Snack emergency," I said weakly.

Her gaze shifted, and her nose screwed up. "What's that smell?"

The pungent scent of rotting river water filled the air. A pile of steaming, stinking coins lay on the floor where the shade had stood.

Killion came to my rescue with an excuse. "A friend fished these out of the lake. He decided to donate them to the clinic."

"Generous," she said, fanning her hand under her nose. "Smells like rotting garbage."

"We'll take them with us and handle the de-stinking process."

"Yeah," I muttered. "We'll take care of them."

She nodded and hurried off.

As soon as she was gone, I shook out my burned hand. "It's getting harder to keep this from her."

I laid the scythe on a dog food bag and grabbed one of our Frosty Paws canvas bags to begin cleaning up the coins.

Killion took the bag from my hands. A wave of his fingers, and the coins disappeared. He examined my burns. "This is serious, Chloe."

Another rare thing—him using my name. The worry flowing off him and into my system ratcheted up my own concern. "I know. I have to figure out a way to rebond with that thing." I cocked my head at the blade. "Otherwise, SMG will confiscate it and lock it away."

A tender and gentle stroke of his hand over mine, and the pain of the burns subsided. A second stroke healed the wounded skin. "Perhaps we should look into that before spending more time researching the Ferryman."

"I need to do both."

He kissed my forehead. "The scythe is your best means of defense. Restoring your connection with it is of utmost importance. Only then can you successfully take on your foes."

"Right." I sighed, staring at it. "So, for now, the plan is simple: Rebond with the scythe, mend the Veil, stop the apocalypse. Piece of cake."

He brushed his thumb over my wrist, causing my pulse to skip. "Did you think it wise to taunt the Ferryman?"

"Wise? No. Strategic? Maybe?"

He quirked a brow. "You have a strategy for stopping him?"

"Not yet, but I've got motivation. I'm not about to let him or Oblivion think I'll cower." I glanced at the spot where the shade and his coin delivery had gone down. "Oblivion sent a message; I sent one back. I wanted to be clear that he isn't welcome in our world."

That rare smile appeared again. "Let's go home and get started on your plan."

I nodded, but when I went to grab the scythe, it vanished.

My blood went cold.

Killion frowned. "Did it just...?"

"Disappear?" A tremor rippled through me as I nodded. "Not on its own, though, I bet." I sighed and met his eyes. Another message had just been sent. "Someone just stole it."

ELEVEN

Late afternoon painted the penthouse in gold and shadow. The scent of river rot clung to my hair and clothes, no matter how many times I scrubbed. It lingered like a curse—proof I'd brushed too close to the Ferryman's river.

I paced the length of the living room while Ghost watched from her bed near the hearth, chin on her paws, eyes tracking every step.

Pennyworth—immaculate as ever in his dark vest and slacks—set down a tray of tea, coffee, and enough scones to feed a small militia. "If you continue to wear a trench in the floor, Mistress, I'll be forced to call the flooring company again."

"Sorry," I muttered, but didn't slow. "I'm stress pacing. Death still hasn't answered."

Pennyworth was always on my side. "He is irksome, but perhaps he's busy. Would ice cream help? I have two of your favorites."

My love of coffee was rivaled only by my addiction to ice cream. "Tempting, but I'm too wired. What's more important than a rip in the Veil and my weapon going MIA? Is he dueling bureaucracy? Preventing the apocalypse? I'd like a heads-up if we're penciled in."

Killion sat in the dining room, the sunlight glazing his cheekbones in gold. He looked entirely composed, legs crossed, a file open in front of him. "Pennyworth's right. Pacing won't summon him faster."

"I'm not pacing. I'm venting kinetically."

His violet gaze lifted, amusement flickering in it. "Your kinetic venting has lasted an hour."

Ghost gave a soft woof.

"Hush," I told her. "You're supposed to be on my side."

Corvus croaked, eyeing a scone. "Kill the vampire."

"Shade," I hurriedly added when Killion lifted a brow. "Kill the vampire *shade*. I already tried that. Technically, he's dead several times over. He's surprisingly durable."

I dropped into the chair opposite Killion, rubbing my palms on my thighs. "I hate this. I feel naked without the scythe."

"That's because it's part of you," he said quietly. "You'll feel the lack until it's returned."

I exhaled hard. "If SMG took it, I swear—"

Pennyworth cleared his throat. "Shall I fetch a bottle of wine, or are we keeping the Void-born sober this evening?"

Void-born—the first reaper and the first blade. Both of us originals, like Death himself.

Killion's mouth curved faintly as he filled a mug with coffee. "This will do for now, thank you."

Once Pennyworth retreated, I reached for the old grimoire I'd brought from Aurora's. The cracked leather cover exhaled dust when I opened it. "Aurora found a section on the First Blade—its forging, its link to the Veil. It says a reaper can rebond through a ritual, but it's vague on the details."

"Read it to me."

"*The bond must be reforged in the place of its birth, under the witness of Death and shadow.*" I glanced up. "That's it. No instructions. No handy bullet points."

Killion rolled his sleeves up to his elbows. The ruby in his ring winked in the sunlight, its twin warming on my finger. Both had been in his family for thousands of years. "It was forged in the Void, like you, Death, and this world."

"And apparently, Oblivion." I looked to him for confirmation. "Right? That's where he hangs out, I presume. Where he originates from?"

A nod. "Diego and I found evidence in the catacombs that suggests our vampire shade was there. Possibly others like him. Coins had been melted into the floors. Some bore runes of passage I've never seen before."

A shiver ran through me. "You think the Ferryman is using them as markers of some sort?"

"We found no sign he's crossed, but the water was

tainted. And Diego swore he heard the echo of oars cutting through water."

"Just like I heard at the cemetery," I muttered. "Great."

He closed the file, meeting my eyes. "The ghost animals, the vampire shade returning, the coins in the catacombs...the Ferryman has his minions entering this world. It won't be long before he's able to use them to materialize."

Shadows stretched long across the floor, bending toward a single point behind me. Death materialized from the darkness, dressed entirely in black. He poured himself a cup of coffee and claimed a scone. "Report."

I jumped up. "What took you so long? What part of *urgent* in the subject line of my message didn't you understand?"

He regarded me coolly, sipping on his coffee as he took a seat at the table. "Some of us have important work to do."

The gall. "Oh, I've been working," I said. "Mostly trying to keep Oblivion from erasing the existence of everything and screwing up the Universal balance. That's your department, remember?"

Killion's low chuckle earned him a glare from both of us.

Death's gaze slid back to me. "You've encountered him?"

"Not him." I recapped quickly about the vampire shade's reappearance, the 'Oblivion eats' message, the scythe burning me—and its disappearance.

The faint amusement drained from his face. He set down his scone, uneaten. "If the weapon refused you again, protocol demands confiscation."

"SMG should have spoken to me first, not snatched it away without a warning."

"Unless they feared you'd refuse to surrender it," Death countered. "Which you already have, and, refresh my memory, but they did warn you they wanted to quarantine it."

"But..." I struggled to counter that fact. "It vanished right in front of my eyes. Just...poof." I made an explosion gesture with my fingers. "A heads-up would have been appreciated."

Killion's voice cut in, smooth but cold. "Unless it wasn't them who took it."

Death's form flickered, a visible shudder of unease. Ever since he'd died and I'd used necromancy to bring him back, his form did this occasionally.

He glanced away from my scrutiny and began to pace, the coffee and scone forgotten. "If Oblivion took it, he's found a breach into this world. But he can't manifest physically. It would require the Ferryman or another corporeal conduit."

"The vampire shade seems likely," I said. "He was bragging about working for the Ferryman and was full of cryptic quips."

Death stopped, eyes narrowing. "Then my seal of the tear at the cemetery hasn't held."

I glanced toward the scythe's holder on its hook. The emptiness of it made me feel hollow inside. Who would have guessed that I'd be so tied to it? "Figured as much, since I've been up to my elbows in ghost animals at the clinic."

Death stopped pacing, shot me a look I couldn't read, and walked to the window without a word.

Corvus croaked, hopping down to walk on the table. He started to peck at Death's abandoned scone, but I shooed him away. He flew up, called me a name, and landed in front of the fireplace. There, he fluffed his wings and strutted about, indignant.

Death glared out the window, where the sunlight struggled against gathering clouds. It matched the expression on his face. "I'll speak with SMG. If they've confiscated the scythe, I'll find a way to retrieve it. If they haven't..." His gaze returned to me, dark as the grave. "Then we prepare for the worst."

"Define worst," I said.

"If the Ferryman wields your blade, he'll rip open the Veil, and we'll have no way to mend it."

He vanished into shadow. The echo of his warning and the sound of Ghost's uneasy whine filled the air.

"I'm not just going to sit here," I said, munching on the scone Death had left behind. "If SMG confiscated my scythe, I'm getting it back myself."

Killion didn't even look up from the file he was closing. "And if they didn't take it?"

"Then I'll find out who did." I turned to face him, crossing my arms. "We should go to Shepherd's Rest. If the Veil's open, maybe I can sense it—maybe the scythe's still connected to it. To me."

His eyes flicked to mine, filled with compassion. "If you can't seal it—which you can't without the scythe—you risk the Ferryman snatching you, too."

"I can borrow Die's scythe. It's not the First Blade, but it is a blade. It might work." Even as I said it, I knew it wouldn't.

He sighed, long-suffering and composed. "I understand your impatience, but that impatience may get you obliterated."

I hated it when he was right. I tossed down the scone. "Then what can I do?"

That earned me a dry, elegant lift of one brow. "Allow me to provide a more civilized distraction."

I knew that tone—seduction disguised as strategy. He rose and crossed to the bar, all quiet grace and lethal calm.

"You're going to get me drunk," I muttered.

He poured two glasses of wine. "Death will handle SMG. Until then, we focus on what we can control."

"Which isn't much." I took the glass he offered.

Killion touched his glass to mine. "To control, however illusory."

"Cheers," I said dryly. "Now tell me what I can do to stop all of this without my blade."

He put an arm around my waist and pulled me to him. His lips brushed my throat, and his words turned cold as stone. "The tunnels were half-flooded," he said, voice low and sexy. "The air was thick with ancient magic. Diego nearly fell over an altar submerged up to its base. It was crusted with salt and fused coins."

I leaned back, pulse quickening—both at his purposeful seduction and this insightful news.

His thumb ghosted along my bottom lip. "I believe it's a shrine—a deliberate attempt to open a portal to the place we least wish him to be."

My stomach turned. I set down my glass, moving away from his wicked lips and possessive hand. "Here."

"Most likely." He took a sip of wine, guiding me to my deserted chair. "The water around it was black and cold. It whispered."

The word hissed in the air between us. "Whispered?" I echoed.

"A strange voice. Not ghost-like. Definitely not human."

A chill crawled up my spine and stayed there.

He reached into his pocket and withdrew a small velvet pouch. "Diego swore he saw something in the reflection—a figure in a rowboat at the edge of the light. When he blinked, it was gone."

I stared at the pouch, already dreading what was inside. "Please tell me you didn't bring home a cursed souvenir."

He smiled faintly. "You wound me."

"I'm serious, Killion. Last time you brought me a gift, it was a haunted dagger. Romantic Gestures, Vampire Edition."

He unwrapped the cloth and revealed a coin—blackened around the edges, shimmering as if wet. Symbols glinted faintly beneath the tarnish.

The moment I touched it, my grim tattoo flared

white-hot, burning through my shirt. I hissed and dropped the coin, the air snapping with dark energy. "Yikes."

Killion rewrapped it and set it on the table. "Same resonance as your scythe?"

My heart sank. "Yes," I said, rubbing the tattoo. The mark pulsed. "The Ferryman's energy is moving through the water. He's clawing his way up from underneath us."

Killion toyed with his glass. "The catacombs connect to the Grove's waterways."

"He's attacking from both sides."

Thunder rumbled outside, low and close. The windows shivered in their frames.

Killion set down his glass and reached for my hand. "You'll need the First Blade to fight him."

I met his gaze, my pulse steadying under the cool slide of his magic against my skin. "Nothing else will do."

He smiled, a dark curve of promise and danger. "If Death fails to retrieve it, we'll have to take certain... measures."

I was about to ask what those might be when a gust of wind howled past the penthouse windows. Ghost lifted her head, ears pricked, staring toward them as if she heard something moving.

Chloe, an eerie, not-human voice called. *Chlooooeeee...*

I whirled, searching for who said it.

No one was there.

But the velvet bag twisted and jerked, the coin inside coming to life.

Chlooooeeee...it whispered. Goose bumps rose all over my skin. *Come to me...*

Killion moved between me and the bag. A dagger appeared in his hand.

Without warning, a soft thump knocked me in the chest. It did it again. I placed a hand there, feeling it pick up the same rhythm as my heartbeat.

Kill. The word echoed in my mind.

"The scythe," I murmured to Killion. "It's...talking to me, like normal. It wants me to kill the coin."

"I feel it," he said. "It's tugging at me through you."

An image of the catacombs flashed across my memory. The tattoo pulsed. "It's calling me."

"To what?"

I met his gaze. "The catacombs."

His jaw tightened. He glanced between me and the bagged coin. "Then that's where we go."

TWELVE

Lightning cracked over the city skyline as we left the penthouse, a jagged vein of light splitting the bruised clouds and catching on a cathedral spire in the distance.

The air smelled coppery, sharp as fresh blood. Wind pushed at us as we reached the service hatch that led into the catacombs. Killion dropped first, graceful even in gloom, then reached up to steady me as I climbed down the ladder with Ghost.

The deeper we went, the thicker the air became. Humidity slicked my skin; every breath tasted like damp stone. Far below the town often referred to as Hell's Rejects, the world smelled of coins and decay—the Ferryman's perfume.

Our footsteps echoed in the dark, syncing with the plink-plink-plink of unseen water.

I tightened my grip on the flashlight. "If it's really the scythe," I whispered, "it's waiting."

Killion's voice carried low behind me, edged in warning. "Or it's bait."

The tunnel seemed to breathe around us, exhaling cold that slid under my collar. Ghost trotted ahead, nose high.

In the dark, something whispered my name again. *Chloeeee....*

The scythe or the Ferryman?

Did you hear that? I asked Killion through the bond.

His reply was tinged with irritation and worry. *I heard it.*

The deeper we descended, the less the world made sense. The tunnel branched, then branched again, until I couldn't tell which direction we were heading—down, sideways, or straight into a river.

My flashlight beam swept across carvings etched into the stone walls. Symbols—half-erased by time and moisture—spiraled in loops that made my eyes ache to follow. Some looked familiar, like the sigils Aurora had shown me in her grimoires. Others pulsed faintly, as though breathing light.

We passed the rooms of crypts, the old monks long ago silenced before being entombed here. Killion trailed one gloved finger over a symbol slick with condensation. "These weren't here earlier."

"That's not reassuring," I muttered. "Either the Ferryman's redecorating, or someone's been trying to open a door they shouldn't."

Ghost nosed at a puddle ahead, whining. Ripples spread outward even though nothing had disturbed the surface. I aimed the flashlight at it, and the beam scattered into dark water that stretched farther than it should have.

The scythe's pull thrummed inside my chest, a steady tug toward the black pool. My grim tattoo flared once—hot, insistent. "It's close."

Killion's voice stayed calm, but I caught the undercurrent beneath it. "You're sure it's not the Ferryman?"

"No," I said. The scythe had been acting so erratically, and I had to be ready for anything. "That's the problem. It feels like my blade, but I can't be sure."

He moved beside me, his presence a quiet shield of power. "Stay close."

"Oh, I am, but it's so I can protect you. Death warned that the Ferryman has an interest in the Undead, remember?" I glanced at him, the beam catching on his sharp jawline and the faint glint of his fangs. "That makes you his favorite snack."

His mouth curved, humorless. "So it would seem."

A sound stirred beyond the water—like the soft drag of oars in silt. The ripples came faster now, pulsing in rhythm with my heartbeat.

Killion's hand brushed mine, fingers gripping mine tightly. "We should turn back."

The tug made my chest hurt; my tattoo burned with urgency. I shook my head. "If my blade is here, I have to retrieve it." I crouched near the edge of the water, the beam cutting a narrow path through the darkness. The reflection trembled—my face, Killion's, Ghost's—and then a shadow moved.

A figure in the water. Cloaked. Rowing. The blade of my scythe glinted in its grasp.

My stomach dropped. "He's here, and he has it."

The Ferryman didn't raise his head, but even from where I stood, I could feel his attention. The air thickened, the moisture in it turning heavy and cold.

Killion hauled me backward, the movement snapping the vision like glass. The water went still. The tunnel's humid, dripping walls returned.

He caught my face between his hands, eyes glowing amethyst. "Did he see you?"

I swallowed hard, the burn of the tattoo fading to an ache. "Oh, yeah," I whispered. "And he smiled."

Killion's grip on me was firm, grounding. "We're leaving," he said. "Now."

"Agreed." I turned toward the tunnel mouth and froze.

A pale shimmer bloomed in the darkness ahead. At first, I thought it was mist rising from the flooded floor. Then it moved.

A woman stepped through it—if 'woman' was even the right word.

Her skin was moonlight, her hair the black of grave soil, cascading in perfect, vintage curls over her bare shoulders. A crimson skirt split to her thigh flowed behind her. Shadows clung to her, whispering and writhing like a living cloak. Two phantoms flanked her, their forms tethered to her wrists by bands of smoke.

Ghost whined, tail low.

Beside me, Killion's posture changed to predatory

stillness and old power. Another layer of his magic snapped into place, protecting us.

"Aveena," he said, his voice bored, but cold and calculating. "You look...unchanged."

Her full lips curved into a smile sharp enough to cut. Her voice purred over the stones, as beautiful as it was lethal. "And you, my love, look deliciously worried. How novel."

My pulse slowed as I reacted to the necrotic energy emanating from her in waves. I tightened my hold on the flashlight, not because I thought it would help, but because it gave my shaking hand a purpose.

The ghoul queen of New Orleans slid her gaze to me, slow and assessing. "Your girl is still alive. Miracles abound."

I bristled. She knew I would. She'd called me the same thing the first time we met. "*Girl?*"

Killion shifted slightly, a silent warning. "I assume you didn't travel from New Orleans to check on us. Why are you here?"

She sighed, feigning disappointment. "No appreciation for theatrics. Very well." Her phantoms snarled behind her, straining at invisible leashes. "I came because you need to know what I've seen."

Her tone changed—smoothness giving way to something harder. "Charon was in my city last night."

Killion went still. I felt his power ripple out, sharp and electric. My own power answered, magnifying it. I shifted so we were shoulder to shoulder as he said, "Impossible. The Veil hasn't breached that far south."

"I saw him with my own eyes." She was still as death, her magic poking fingers at mine. She couldn't get past Killion's bubble of protection, or my own shield, but she enjoyed playing with us. "He came to my graveyard. Dristan LeBihan and I were discussing...rights to a new burial ground outside the French Quarter." Her expression turned grave. "Charon took Dristan."

Killion had told me about Dristan LeBihan—one of the oldest masters in the southern covens. His vampires stretched across half the Gulf states.

"What do you mean by *took*?" I asked.

"I mean," she said softly, "Death's ferryman took him. You, of all people, shouldn't need me to draw you a diagram."

"The Ferryman doesn't work for Death," I countered. "He's not one of us."

Her head tilted, a brow quirking. "But he is. He reaps souls."

"For Oblivion," I said. "Not Soul Management Group."

Her ruby red lips pursed. "Oblivion?"

Killion's tone remained steely. "Have you not heard of him?"

Her phantoms writhed. She frowned. "No."

I gave her a lightning-fast rundown, and her frown deepened, marring her near-perfect face. "Within hours of Dristan's abduction, the vampires he'd sired...died," she told us. "As in *truly died*. They bled out and turned to dust."

The air went razor-thin. Killion's face remained

composed, but his aura flared, brushing mine with waves of fury. "All of them?"

Aveena nodded. "All of those in New Orleans. I saw some of them myself. They fell like marionettes with their strings cut. Their blood boiled out of them as if the bond were dissolved."

"If Oblivion erased Dristan, then..." I started.

Killion finished the thought. "He unmade those Dristan sired."

Aveena shook her head. "But they weren't unmade to return to humanity—they were left as corpses— empty, rotting corpses. Even I wouldn't touch the remains."

I grabbed Killion's hand. "If Oblivion can erase a master vampire *and* his line..."

"Then all vampires are vulnerable," Killion finished grimly.

Aveena's dark eyes glittered. "And your sanctuary here—this nest of tragic, lost souls—is filled with many who don't even know who sired them. If Oblivion reaches for the wrong thread, they'll vanish before you can blink. Tragic, isn't it?"

Silence pressed close. Even the dripping water had gone still.

"So that's the game," I murmured. "Oblivion's not just feeding on souls. He's erasing history. If Dristan never existed, his line was never turned. The world rearranges itself to fill the gap."

Aveena smiled faintly. "Now you begin to understand why I came."

Killion moved a step forward. "You risked a great deal leaving your territory unguarded."

Her eyes softened. "Some debts transcend territory." She pinned him with her dead, yet soulful, eyes. "Be careful, my king. He's hunting those who stand between life and death."

Her attention flicked to me, her smile sharpening again. "And you, little reaper—you're practically made of that contradiction. Keep your scythe close."

With a whisper of silk and shadow, Aveena dissolved into mist, her revenants fading with her.

The tunnel was silent once more.

My stomach churned. Killion wasn't an ordinary master. He was born of the Originals—the first beings who became trapped here from another dimension and birthed the vampire race. "If he erases you or your father..." Again, I couldn't finish the statement, my stomach now in my throat.

"Then the only original bloodline left ceases to exist." His gaze was still fixed on the spot where Aveena had stood. "All vampires will die."

My heart thudded hard. "And each one of them in Dante's Grove just ran out of time."

My flashlight's reflection on the flooded floor guttered, and for a moment, I thought the Ferryman had returned.

Then the shadows folded, and Death stormed out of them. His coat snapped behind him like a banner of midnight, his face drawn tight with something I rarely saw on him—rage. The scythe was in his hand, its silver edge burning through the gloom.

"My blade," I breathed. My pulse skipped, and sweat broke out along my hairline. "What—? How? You got it back from the Ferryman?"

He held the weapon out to me. "Take it, and no, he didn't have it."

I blinked, disbelieving, turning back toward the water. "But I saw him with it."

"An illusion." His voice was flint and thunder, echoing through the catacomb. "The fools at SMG locked it in containment after it burned you. They said you were compromised." His eyes cut to me, hard and frustrated. "I disagreed."

My heart lurched as I hesitated to touch the blade. What if it rejected me again? "You stole it? You, Death himself, went against SMG protocol?"

"I went against their cowardice," he snarled. "They were debating authorization while Oblivion's rot spreads through the Veil. Bureaucracy won't save the world."

He thrust the scythe toward me again. I hesitated, then reached for it. The moment I touched it, white fire leaped from the blade and raced up my arm. My tattoo flared, and the familiar hum—painful and intimate—coursed through me.

I held my breath. The bond felt...*alive* again. But what if...?

Reading my thoughts, Killion's hand pressed lightly at my back, his voice low. "We'll figure out the spell. All will be well."

"I don't even want to know," Death said. His gaze

snapped to me. "Your wolf. The one who lost his magic. He's at Shepherd's Rest."

My stomach cramped from the tone of his voice. "And?"

Death's tone dropped to something like a growl. "He's in trouble. He needs you."

The blade hummed in my palm. The skin there warmed, but didn't burn. It felt...normal.

"How fast can we get there?" I asked.

Death put a hand on each of our shoulders, and the three of us went tumbling through space.

THIRTEEN

We materialized on the edge of Shepherd's Rest. The night was too still for comfort, only the wind swirling through the iron gate, rattling the chains like restless bones.

The faint glow of lights flickered between rows of crooked headstones. At first, I thought they were spirit lights—until I heard laughter.

A group of tourists gathered near the chapel ruin, cameras out, breath pluming in the cold. And at the center of them—looking perfectly, painfully normal—was Andy.

He wore his worn leather jacket, ball cap turned backward, a flashlight in one hand as he gestured toward a headstone and recited a well-practiced joke. His voice was steady, and his audience laughed again.

Relief flooded me so fast it hurt. "He's fine," I whispered. "He's just working."

Death's tone was flat. "Appearances deceive."

Ghost barked. I ignored my boss, taking a step forward and waving. "Andy!"

He turned in our direction, surprise crossing his face. "Chloe? What are you doing here?" His gaze snagged on Death, and his face fell. He begged off from the group to join us, lowering his voice. "You brought the circus. What's going on?"

Killion's expression stayed carved from marble. "This *circus* is here to warn you."

Andy's brow furrowed. He shoved his free hand in his jacket pocket. "What now?"

The ground trembled, and a whisper crawled through the fog. The tourists stopped laughing. One pointed toward a grave, mouth slack.

I turned—and my heart stopped.

A pale figure rose from the earth, not a full body, just a shape of mist and bone. Then another and another.

Ghosts, and lots of them. "The Veil is open again," I muttered. The air shimmered with cold, spectral light. "Andy, you need to cancel this tour. Now."

He looked around, color draining from his face. "I—I don't—"

"Do it!" Death snapped.

Andy fumbled with his flashlight, hurrying back to the tour group. Never losing his humor, he rounded them up, using some excuse about a gas leak, and the tourists began backing away. I hid my scythe behind my back while Killion stood next to me as they departed. Death, who rarely let mortals see him, stood on my other side, the three of us a wall.

Their nervous laughter drifted off as the bus hauled them away, but my anxiety turned to panic as the ghosts solidified—flickering men, women, children, some ancient, some fresh from the grave. As we faced them, they formed rows among the headstones and mausoleums, facing us like an army of the dead.

"Death," I hissed, "do something."

His gaze swept the horde. "I believe that's your job. You're the one with the blade."

My grip on the scythe's handle tightened. My palm heated uncomfortably. "There are too many," I said. "They're flooding through."

Andy slid up next to Killion. "I see them." It was said with a tinge of awe. When he'd lost his magic, he'd lost many abilities, seeing ghosts had been one of them.

"Because whoever called them wants them to be visible," Death said. He sighed audibly, fingers twitching at his side. "We have to close the rip again."

The scythe trembled, straining with the pull of so many lost souls. My tattoo burned like fire under my shirt. "We'd better do it fast."

Ghosts filled the cemetery and even clustered in the naked tree branches, hanging like pale fruit. Their whispers grew loud, a thousand voices overlapping.

"Andy, you stay here," I told him.

Since I was the only one with a scythe, I had to take the lead. There was no other way to send the ghosts back to where they came from. I strode forward, raising the blade, ready to start swinging. Killion and Death stayed right on my heels.

The ghosts didn't stay in place—not that I thought they would. Instead of attacking, though, they parted before me. Every time I lunged for one of them, they faded out, only to flicker back into being somewhere farther along.

"Stop," Killion growled. "They're driving you to that crypt."

He was right. I pulled up short. "Where is the rip?" I searched the air above the spectral heads, ignoring those in the trees. I used the tip of the blade to point. "It was over there last time."

I didn't think it was possible for Death to be closer than Killion, but he was nearly breathing down my neck. "This way."

He drove the ghosts out of the way as we stepped over and around raised beds. Some refused to move, still trying to steer us in the other direction, but I sliced them down. Point made, the others continued evading me, and we finally reached the far crypt.

The air turned to liquid ice. A slit of darkness shimmered above the ground, the wound oozing a thick, watery liquid that smelled of rot.

Death muttered several curses under his breath. "It's worse than the last one."

Before I could respond, the fog thickened, and the scythe burned.

The Ferryman emerged, cloaked in black, coins glinting where his eyes should have been.

"Get behind me," Killion ordered.

"No," I said instantly. "You're the one in the most danger. You have to leave."

He shot me a look that could cut glass. "Not happening."

Death moved forward, power radiating in waves. "You dare trespass in my territory?"

The Ferryman tilted his head, and his voice rolled like the tide—slow, deep, mocking. "Not your territory anymore." His gaze slid past him to land on me. Paused. "The Grim."

The way he said it was formal. He knew me as the original—Grim Zero.

I straightened ever so slightly and gave him the classic Killion glare. "You don't belong in this world, and I'm going to send you back," I told him.

Smug amusement toyed around his thin lips. "You'll be mine soon enough." And then his gaze slid to a spot behind me.

I glanced back and frowned. Andy. "I told you to stay back."

Andy's throat worked. "I'm not leaving you. I'm not... helpless."

"You've lost something precious," the Ferryman said to him. "Magic that once sang in your blood." Water pooled around his feet, a tide coming in. "I can return it to you."

Chills crawled down my arms. What was he talking about?

Andy laughed shakily. "Sure you can. And I'm the Tooth Fairy."

A part of me wanted to rush forward and swing my blade as hard as I could. Killion sensed it and wrapped his fingers around my wrist. "Don't listen to him," I muttered to Andy. "He doesn't have that kind of magic. None of us do."

From the fog beside the Ferryman, a new shape formed. I knew her instantly—Carmen Santos, the witch shade. Her eyes were hollow sockets of pale flame.

"She can give it back," the Ferryman said.

"That's impossible," I hissed. I glanced at my boss. Death was stoic, studying both the Ferryman and Carmen's ghost. "Right?"

Carmen lifted her hand and whispered something in an archaic language. A sphere of light formed between her palms—blinding and beautiful, pulsing with magic.

Andy froze. His eyes reflected it, wide and hungry.

"No." I lifted the blade, trying to draw his attention. "Andy, don't—"

The witch flicked her wrist. The light shot forward and struck him in the chest.

He convulsed, arched. A sound tore from his throat— half scream, half howl. The air crackled with power. His eyes glowed amber for a heartbeat—then the light vanished. Carmen drew it back, the light ball spinning in her cupped hands.

Andy dropped to his knees, gasping.

I tore away from Killion and Death, running to him. "Andy!"

The Ferryman chuckled, low and pleased. "So easy, isn't it? To crave what's gone."

"Leave him alone!" I kneeled beside Andy. His body trembled under my hands.

The Ferryman's smile was all hunger. "I can make you whole again, wolf. All you must do is one small thing for me."

Andy's head lifted, sweat and dirt streaking his face. He gasped like he'd run a mile full out in human form. "What?"

I couldn't tell if he was shocked by the offer or truly curious. Maybe both.

Losing his magic had nearly killed him. Emotionally. Mentally. It had gutted him in ways I couldn't begin to fathom. Still, this was an empty promise. A carrot dangling on a stick. I shook him. "No, Andy. You can't trust him!"

The ghosts tightened their circle around us, hundreds of them, their hollow eyes reflecting the moon's glow.

"Bring me the reaper's blade," the Ferryman whispered, but it carried across the graveyard, echoing as if amplified by all of his spectrals. "That's all."

Andy's gaze flicked toward my scythe. For a single, terrifying second, his sole focus was on the scythe. A keen concentration that I read as the intent to do precisely that.

Of course, the Ferryman would offer him the one thing he wanted more than anything else. It was probably the one and only thing that might turn him against me.

"No." I stumbled back. Even if he *did* try to take it from me, he couldn't. He was no longer a supernatural; I was. A very strong, very powerful one. Plus, I had Killion and Death backing me up. "Don't even think about it. You can't—and you won't—take it from me."

Death's voice rang out like thunder. "Enough. Werewolf, get out of here. Chloe, reap the souls."

The ghosts screamed—and rushed us.

I swung.

The world exploded in light and wind and screaming spirits. The first ghost hit me like ice water. Its touch ripped through flesh and bone, leaving my nerves singing with cold fire. Another slammed into the shield Killion rose around us and shattered like glass, its pieces whirling into mist that cut the air like shards.

"Keep moving!" Death's voice thundered through the chaos. He swept his arm, sending a black shockwave through the nearest specters. They screamed, tearing apart midair, but more poured in to take their place.

Ghost barked wildly, snapping at the wraiths as they swarmed closer. Andy staggered to his feet, his eyes flickering between gold and blue. "What—what's happening—?"

"The Veil's vomiting souls," I shouted. The scythe burned white-hot in my hand, pulling, wanting. I swung.

The blade cut through three spirits at once, the air splitting open with a hiss. Each ghost dissolved in a burst of silver ash. Power surged through me, bright and terrible, and the voices of the dead howled inside my skull.

"More behind you!" Killion shouted.

I spun. A cluster of them rushed him—human shapes that weren't quite solid, eyes like hollow moons. He drew his daggers, moving faster than light, but their cold hands clawed at his coat, tearing fabric, reaching for the heat of his pulse.

"No!" I shouted, slicing through the ghosts. I hit a wall of them, and the impact threw me against a headstone, pain lancing through my shoulder.

Death appeared beside me, his cloak snapping like a storm. "Focus, Grave Girl. You're drawing on the Veil itself—control it!"

Drawing on the Veil... It was pulsing through me, and I hadn't even noticed. Could I control it? "How?" I slashed again, the scythe's arc spilling light that tore through the darkness. The Ferryman's laughter rolled through the graveyard, deep and resonant, like the toll of a drowned bell.

He was everywhere and nowhere. Every gust of wind carried his voice.

"You can't fight the tide, Reaper."

The ground split under my boots, and a wave of ghostly hands clawed up from the soil. One wrapped around my ankle, cold and relentless. I brought the blade down hard, severing it, only for two more to take its place.

Killion moved to cover me, his fangs flashing, eyes burning amethyst. He drove a dagger into the ground and murmured an ancient command. Power flared outward— a dome of shadowed energy that shredded the closest spirits like smoke in the wind.

The Ferryman's shape flickered in the distance, his oars dragging across invisible water that rippled through the air itself. Beside him, Carmen raised her arms, chanting in a voice that was both scream and song.

"Not again," I growled. "Not another spell."

I sprinted forward, cutting through a wall of spirits. The scythe blazed, leaving trails of white fire in the air. Each swing sent shockwaves of energy that rattled tombstones and blew open crypt doors. The smell of rot and decay filled my lungs.

I didn't head for the witch or the Ferryman—I went for the Veil.

My blade sizzled as I pressed it against the oozing liquid. The air quivered. The ghosts screamed.

Another explosion shook the cemetery. Ghosts scattered like leaves. The witch shade shrieked as her body fractured into threads of shadow. The Ferryman reached for her, his face—or what passed for one—distorting with fury.

Then he vanished, pulling her with him, the echo of a roar curling through the wind.

My breath came ragged, the scythe heavy and hot in my grip. The air still shimmered with fading souls drifting upward like sparks from a dying fire. When the last ghost dispersed, silence fell like ash.

"Killion?" I turned, heart hammering hard enough to drown out the wind. "Killion—?"

"There," Andy rasped, voice shredded. Blood streaked his face, his hands shaking as he pointed. "He was right there, and then—"

I followed his gaze. My knees hit the dirt before I

realized I'd fallen. A thin puddle of silver water trembled on top of a grave in the shape of my husband, my soul mate.

It rippled once, then stilled and turned to ice.

FOURTEEN

Killion was gone.

The silver puddle's ice reflected nothing. No sky. No me. Only the kind of black void that eats light.

My chest stuttered. Even the air around me felt wrong—thin, brittle, like the world was holding its breath. I was certainly holding mine.

Ghost nudged my hand, and I absentmindedly petted her. The headstone caught my attention. My insides further bombed out. *Gertrude Grace Elizabeth Reveux, adored wife. Marius Cipriam Reveux, cherished son—* Killion's human wife and son. The ones who'd died from influenza in the 1920s.

Had he seen their ghosts? Had they crossed the Veil and tempted him, whispering for him to join them? Was that why he'd been at this grave? A trick, no doubt, by the Ferryman to trap him.

To erase him.

A sob caught in my throat. I touched the soulless ice,

tears running down my cheeks. The moon overhead reflected on my blade. "He's gone," I said hoarsely. "The Ferryman...erased him."

Which meant Marius had never existed. Which meant neither had boy's laughter Killion had told me about, nor the toy soldiers Marcus loved to play with.

Death's shadow loomed beside me. "If he had, the grave marker would not bear Killion's son's name. If he had, you wouldn't still be breathing."

I stood and whipped around, dashing the tears off my cheeks. The thought took a heartbeat to sink in. *He's right.* "*Incatusa sufletum*," I whispered—the soul mate bond that intertwined our lives.

He flicked dirt off his coat. "If he were truly erased from existence, the tether between you would have snapped—and dragged you into nothing right alongside him."

My pulse hammered, even as relief swamped me. "He's alive."

"Technically, no, he's still Undead, but he's in existence somewhere," Death said. "Somewhere beyond this world. Beyond reach."

"Not beyond mine." I pressed my palm to my chest and sank inward, diving past the hum of my own magic, past Grim Zero, as I searched for my soul mate's essence. Usually, our link was as easy to tap into as my own heartbeat. Now, it was there, but so faint and flickering it took me a minute to be sure it wasn't a phantom. But it was real, a thready pulse that couldn't find a steady rhythm.

Killion, I sent through the connection. *Are you okay?*

The bond remained quiet, cold, and brittle. What felt like wind buffeted against my mind. An icy thread of magic tried to freeze my blood. I brushed it aside and kept sinking farther, pushing through the barriers.

The connection fractured like a frozen lake, splintering in all directions. I gasped and fell back, clutching at my heart. "Reapers," I hissed. "He's there—I can feel him—but every step toward him is like walking into a blizzard made of ice knives."

Death folded his arms. "He's on the other side in the Ferryman's in-between world."

The Ghost Lands. My gut twisted, arguments formed. "The Ferryman can't keep him in the Ghost Lands for long. I mean, I know he's Undead, but even so, he's not a ghost. What if..." My mind whirled. "What if they're in the catacombs? We saw evidence that the Ferryman had been there, and Caleb's drawings included that place. It's another way for him to enter our world—I just don't know exactly how he's doing it."

Death gave me that *you're grasping at ghosts* look. "Unlikely."

"Maybe." Annoyance and impatience warred inside me. The clock was ticking. "But I need to be sure."

I pulled out my phone with shaking fingers and texted Harlow and Katarina.

Killion's missing. Taken by the Ferryman. Check the catacombs. Be careful.

The moment I hit send, a voice broke through the quiet. "Dr. Frost?"

I turned. Caleb stood at the edge of the path with his

parents. He clutched a sketchbook to his chest. His big eyes were wide, solemn, and old in a way that made my heart ache.

Ghost ran to the boy, who bent to pet her. I slide the scythe out of sight. Caleb's father nodded at Andy and held out a page to me. "He drew this just moments ago. We thought you should see it. Look at the moon."

Charcoal lines formed an image that stopped my heart—a man lying on the ground in a graveyard, reaching for a scythe. His face was pale, shadowed, but I knew that jawline, that hand.

Killion.

Above him, a full moon blazed like a silver eye.

My gaze flicked upward. The real moon hung fat and bright, not quite full—but close. A day, maybe two, until it would peak?

A tremor of hope sparked in my chest. Hope was dangerous—it had teeth—but I clung to it anyway. "If this is a prophecy, then we have time to save him." I glanced at Caleb and his parents. "Thank you. Can I keep this?"

Caleb nodded, and his parents guided him away. I stared at the drawing while more thoughts tangled in my head. A full moon in two days...Halloween.

I examined the landscape around Killion's sketched form. The corner of the raised grave made me pause and look over my shoulder at the real thing. I crouched near Eliza and Marius' grave. The silver pool of water had disappeared, leaving only a thin silver outline—like the ghost of his body drawn in moonlight.

It was reaching for something, just like in the drawing. But my scythe hadn't been here...

I glanced up at the moon again, fearing that maybe the drawing was in error—that Caleb had been seeing tonight, not the future. But my scythe had never been near Killion. I brushed a thumb over Killion's face on the paper. "I'll find you, wherever you are."

Aurora appeared at the gates, skirts swirling, hair unbound. She ran down the path and over the split ground, heading straight for Andy.

He stood apart from Death and me, rubbing his chest as if something ached inside it.

"Are you all right?" she breathed.

He didn't meet her eyes. "Fine." His gaze lifted toward the moon, throat working as if remembering what it had felt like when he'd howled.

Aurora's expression tightened. She strode over to me. "What happened?"

I told her about the ghost army, the Ferryman, the witch shade, and the offer of magic.

Her face drained of color. "There's no spell to bring back his magic," she insisted. "I've told him that."

"Carmen put on a good show. It must have felt real enough to him." I nodded his way and folded the drawing. "I'm sorry, I can't help with that right now. Killion's..." My throat closed up.

She searched my face and then the graveyard, looking for him. "Where is he?"

"The Ferryman got him," Andy said, striding past us and down the slope, shoulders hunched.

"Got him? Oh, Chloe, I'm so sorry."

I wrestled up some bravado I didn't feel. "I'm going to find him and get him back."

Aurora hesitated, torn, then pressed a thick leather-bound tome into my hands. "I think I know what the Ferryman's up to. On Halloween, there's a Grave Moon —a rare convergence of planets while the Veil is at its thinnest. He plans to use it."

My breath caught. The full moon.

She opened the book to a marked page. The ink shimmered, alive with an old enchantment. Death stepped beside me, reading over my shoulder.

I read the ornate script aloud. *"The Grave Moon opens the passage between worlds and strengthens those who dwell beyond the Veil."*

Aurora nodded grimly. "It will supercharge them. The Ferryman, the ghosts, anything waiting to cross—it'll give them the power to do it."

Death's tone dropped an octave. "And allow Oblivion to pass through and claim this world."

The words made the ground seem to tilt, like the world itself didn't want to hear them. I shut the book with a snap. My phone buzzed in my pocket. It was Harlow.

No sign of Killion. Catacombs are clear.

My stomach turned. "We have to find Killion. That's our first priority."

Death raised a haughty brow. "Saving the world is our first priority."

I met his gaze, the scythe heavy in my grip. "If Oblivion erases Killion, it'll erase me. And possibly this."

I held it up. "That might've been his plan all along. Without the scythe, you can't fix the Veil. Without the Veil, there's no world left to save."

Death stared at me for a long beat, then sighed like the weight of every century he'd ever lived was pressing on his shoulders. "You're infuriating, but I have to admit, your argument is sound."

"Thanks," I said. "I practice at being both annoying and right."

He rolled his eyes, grabbed my shoulder, and whistled for Ghost. "Let's go find Fang Boy before the world ends."

The cemetery vanished in a rush of wind and dark.

FIFTEEN

Crossing into the Veil usually felt like slipping through silk—cold, whisper-thin, and strangely weightless.

This time, it felt like drowning in rotting velvet.

The shadows peeled back in streaks of gray and silver, bleeding into each other with sickening ease. The air was thick, wet, and heavy. Every breath tasted like rust and grave dirt.

My boots hit solid ground—never had that happen before. Usually, the Ghost Lands were groundless, leaving me weightless and unanchored. This terrain squelched like mud, and when I looked down, it was moving—slow ripples crawling under the surface as if worms moved under the Veil.

Ghost barked the second her paws touched the ground. Her hackles stood straight up, tail low, head swiveling toward the unseen things shifting beyond the fog. "Easy, girl," I whispered, though my own pulse was hammering. She wasn't wrong to be spooked.

The Ghost Lands were eerie, ghost-laden, and unsafe. The spirits lingering here hated reapers, often blaming us for ending their lives, even though their soul contracts had expired.

Now, the place was devoid of them, strangely quiet. All I could hear was an odd drone, like hundreds of voices moaning in unison—a hive of bees inside my skull.

The light wasn't white-gray like usual, either. It glowed a pinkish-red, like diluted blood. The air itself shimmered, and tiny motes of silver light drifted past, flickering in and out of existence.

I reached out and touched one. A soundless, psychic wail tore through my skull and vanished before I could pull my hand back. I staggered, clutching my temple. "Okay," I gasped. "That's different."

Death, next to me, had winced at it as well, telling me he'd heard it, too. "Something's wrong."

Ya think? "Glad we're all caught up," I said, trying for humor but barely managing a rasp.

He scanned the shifting horizon. Jagged spires of bone had replaced the normal ghostly expanse of mist, each weeping silver fluid that ran into deep channels cut through the soil. The streams twisted together in the distance, glinting faintly. "Are those...rivers?"

"Not rivers." He crouched to trail a finger through the fluid. It clung to him like mercury, then dripped off and sank into the ground. "Veinlines. The Veil's lifeblood. It's being poisoned."

The scythe quivered, a low buzz rising from its blade. Its silver edge shifted between light and shadow. That was new, too. It strained against my grip, trying to tug me forward.

Ghost pressed against my leg, whining. "Yeah, I feel it too," I whispered. "It's pulling us somewhere."

Death's head snapped up. "The blade is responding?"

"Are you surprised?" The tattoo burned, and I could almost hear the blade whispering—soft, indistinct words beneath the buzz. *Come. Kill.* The words slithered down my spine, half command, half craving. I allowed it to rise, like a divining rod. "It wants me to go that way."

Shadows gathered in my boss's eyes. He glanced in that direction, his hands fisting at his sides. "Seems dangerous."

"So is standing still." I started walking. Each step sank into the soft, rippling ground, releasing faint sighs from below.

Death followed, reluctant but silent, Ghost trotting along between us. The fog shifted around us, curling in slow, sentient eddies.

I expected Death to feel at ease here, even if we were trying to stop Oblivion. His tense expression and set jaw told me he was as worried as I was. "This place mirrors the corruption in the living world," he said.

"Where are all the ghosts?"

"Already erased. The Ferryman gathers them; Oblivion feeds."

I shivered, tightening my grip on the scythe.

Ahead, the mist thickened—dense, veined with that

same silver-red glow. The scythe tugged harder, throbbing in rhythm with my pulse. Ghost barked a warning sound, and I swore I saw shapes dragging themselves across the ground, dissolving before I could focus on them.

"A few still remain," I whispered. "But they're... wrong."

Death didn't argue. "This whole place is corrupted. You should turn back. If Killion is here, I'll find him."

"Not happening."

A faint wind rose, and with it, the drone of voices did too, whispering through the haze. I froze.

Reaper... wrooong side... The words warped mid-syllable. *Run while youuu can...*

I turned, searching for the source, and sucked in a breath. The fog was now full of faces—half-formed, half-melted, watching us from the edges. Every one of them glowed red, not the usual pale gray of the dead.

Ghost growled, teeth bared.

"They're afraid," Death said quietly. "They know what's waiting for them."

My skin crawled. "Oblivion."

Saying the name seemed to thicken the air. The scythe gave a violent pulse, nearly jerking from my grip. A flare of silver light slashed through the fog ahead, like lightning—but it didn't fade. It stayed, throbbing, beckoning.

Whatever waited beyond that silver light was calling me and the scythe—and my blade was hungry.

It dragged me forward, a compass needle locked on

doom. Every few steps, it twitched, impatient, craving. The fog parted to reveal a slope leading down into a hollow where the light turned liquid, and the ground sank. The air reeked of mildew and rotting flowers left too long on a grave.

A river ran through the hollow, silver-black, thick as mercury and slow as tar. Faint red veins flickered beneath the surface. Each throb sent ripples of cold up my legs.

"Tell me that's not blood," I said.

Death's expression was unreadable. "Not exactly. Souls decay, just like flesh. This is their runoff."

My stomach turned. The chill crawled higher, freezing my chest. I swallowed bile. "You're saying we're standing in the soul equivalent of a septic tank?"

"Charming as always."

I huffed and scanned the banks. "If sarcasm were armor, I'd be invincible."

Jagged ribs of bone jutted from the mire, forming what might once have been a dock. Dozens of splintered poles lay in the mud. Carved into the nearest post, barely visible beneath a crust of ash, were symbols I didn't recognize.

The scythe's blade flashed, spilling light across the water. The reflection elongated and shrank. It didn't mirror me, or Death, or even Ghost. It showed movement —a shadow struggling under the surface.

The soul bond kicked hard inside my chest. I dropped to my knees, heart slamming against my ribs. "Killion?"

His name barely left my lips before the water shivered. For one impossible instant, a face appeared—pale, beautiful, furious. His. He was reaching up, eyes set with determination. I felt my name echo through the bond, as if he'd heard me. *Chloe.*

I plunged a hand toward the water, but Death grabbed my wrist. "Don't. It's not him."

The darkness swallowed Killion's face, and the bond froze in silent protest. I jerked my wrist from Death's grip. My body shook from anger. I nearly smacked him. "That was *him.* I felt the bond."

"It was an illusion." Death's tone was sharp, cold. He grabbed me by the shoulders, locking eyes with me. "Oblivion is a master at it. I have no doubt that Fang Boy is here, but *that* wasn't him. This river is bait. Oblivion knew you would come for him. If you touch that water, the Ferryman will drag you under, too."

My heart sank. "Then where is he? How do I find him?"

The water churned, and a bubble of silver light rose, bursting into a whisper that slithered through my mind.

You owe me. It's time you paid your debt.

The words crawled beneath my skin. Whose voice was that? The Ferryman's? Oblivion's?

The ground trembled. From the shallows, something began to crawl out. At first I thought it was a corpse, but it was worse—a lattice of bones fused together, sinew made of shadow. Dozens of faces pressed against the surface, mouths gaping in soundless agony. The air reeked of wet iron.

The scythe vibrated violently in my hand. "What in the grave is that?"

"A Sentinel," Death said. "A guardian of the river and the Ferryman's enforcer."

It dragged itself fully onto the bank, towering above us as it stood, dripping spectral filth. Its many mouths opened and spoke as one. *The Reaper's debt must be paid.*

Shock and disgust shivered through me. "Pretty sure my tab's current," I muttered, raising my scythe.

Kill, it hissed. The word pulsed inside my skull, echoing the blade's hunger.

Death drew his own weapon, a curve of darkness that shimmered. He twirled the blade once with an ease that came from practice. "Let's dispatch this monstrosity back to Oblivion."

The Sentinel lunged. The scythe met its blow, sparks of raw soul-energy exploding around us. The recoil rattled my bones, the noise it made sounding like a bell tolling.

The thing shrieked, and pressure crushed against my eardrums. Ghost morphed, snarling, teeth flashing as she snapped at the creature's trailing shadows.

Killion's face—illusion or not—flashed through my mind. I swung again, channeling everything I had. The blade sliced through one of the Sentinel's arms. Light burst from the wound—tiny souls spilling free like fireflies, fleeing upward toward the dark sky.

The creature recoiled, trembling, its form flickering. Death struck low, severing the chains binding it to the river.

The Sentinel dissolved, all the faces and screams folding into a point of blackness.

I lowered the scythe, breath shaking. The symbols on the dock blazed once, then faded, leaving a single phrase scorched into the bone.

SANCTUM MORTIS – ANCHOR POINT ONE

Death straightened, frowned. "He's opening gateways. Each one is tied to a different Sanctum."

"What's a Sanctum?"

"Soul Management Group constructs—dimensional stabilizers built to regulate the flow of souls between realms. Think of them like keystones in the bridge between life and death. Every region has one. Didn't you read about them in your Grim Manual?"

The manual my psychopomp dog ate and that I'd had to get a replacement for? Gripping stuff, there. "Refresh my memory."

"They were once holy places of passage, but over time, Smudgy shut them down. They couldn't handle the load of souls passing into and out of life anymore."

"Who knew overpopulation affects the afterlife, too?" He grunted, not appreciating my sarcasm. "Why didn't SMG lock them up or destroy them?" I asked.

"They sealed them." He tucked his weapon away and started walking. "Obviously, their duct tape didn't hold."

Sarcasm met with sarcasm. At least it kept me from dissolving in a puddle. "What do we do now?"

"Sever the anchors and restore the balance."

"And find Killion."

He gave an aggrieved tilt of his head. "And that."

I stared into the dark river, and beneath its surface, I swore I saw Killion again—faint, defiant, still fighting.

There was no tug on the soul bond, this time, though. Was it only an illusion?

"Hold on," I whispered to him. "I'm coming."

SIXTEEN

The deeper we went, the more wrong the Ghost Lands seemed. I wasn't even sure if these truly were the Ghost Lands. "This doesn't feel like it did on previous trips," I said to Death. "It was never so...solid."

"The anchors are active again." He stomped over a jagged rock. "They make it less ethereal and far more dangerous."

The air pressed close and heavy, thick as storm water. The gravity was oppressive, dragging on my legs. The fog was alive, pulsing, every beat releasing a faint, wet hiss.

The scythe's guiding hum dropped lower, almost a growl. Each vibration crawled up my arm and into my chest, syncing with my heartbeat until I couldn't tell which was which.

Ghost padded beside me, paws leaving no prints on the ground. She was back in puppy form, her psychopomp form demanding more energy than this realm could give. Head low and ears back, she didn't even sniff at the terrain. She stumbled over a small ridge of bone that jutted from the path.

"Hey," I murmured, crouching beside her. "You okay, girl?"

Her fur rippled under my hand, flickering between solid and smoke. She gave a low whimper, the sound dissolving into static.

"What's happening?" Panic edged into my voice. I set down the scythe and clutched her to me. She didn't fight my grip, her body limp in my arms.

Death, who'd kept walking, stopped and pivoted. "She's been here too long." He studied my face. "You have too. You're both fading. If we don't find anything in the next few minutes, I have to get you out, regardless."

Fading? He made it sound... life-threatening. "But she can't—"

"Die?" Death interrupted, tone unreadable. "No. But she can be unmade."

I turned on him. "Unmade?"

He didn't look at me. His gaze swept the endless horizon, where the fog thickened to a bruised reddish hue. "The balance of this place is inverted. What feeds spirits here now starves them. The Ferryman's corruption leeches everything—will, memory, energy."

The weight of that truth settled over me, a riptide stealing my breath. I glanced down at Ghost, her breathing shallow, her form flickering. My chest ached.

"Rest," I whispered to her. "Stay with me."

She pressed her nose to my palm, and her eyes brightened. But it was brief. Her head nestled against my chest as she panted. She trusted me to fix this.

Could I? That same exhaustion wanted to drown me. Even standing took effort. I grabbed my weapon, my magic heavier in my veins, sluggish, like wading through mud. "A few minutes isn't enough time. I can't stop looking for Killion."

Death gave another of those overly dramatic and impatient sighs. "The Ghost Lands are no place for the living. You know that."

My voice wobbled. "There has to be something you can do."

The scythe gave a sharp jolt in my hand. Death and I exchanged a look. As it pulled, I followed, praying it might be leading me to Killion. Around a bend in the bone path, the fog glowed brighter, redder.

The soul bond fluttered weakly, and I hugged Ghost tighter. "I feel him. Whatever's ahead is pulling on Killion, too."

Death's eyes darkened. "Let's hope it's not an illusion."

We kept moving—three shadows slipping through a dying world. The fog began to thin. What had been a blank wall of red gloom became translucent, showing movement behind it. Pale figures drifted just out of sight, as though walking behind glass. They didn't wail or moan the way ghosts usually did. They whispered.

I slowed, lifting the scythe. "They're watching us."

Death made no move to draw his weapon. "They see your light."

"My—what?"

"Your signature." His tone was clinical, detached, but his eyes weren't. "Reapers burn bright in the Veil. You've walked here enough times that your imprint lingers."

I swallowed, pulse quickening. "That doesn't sound like a good thing."

"They think you can save them," he said.

Ghost gave a low, uncertain growl, her head turning as one of the shapes broke through the mist and stepped closer. It was small—child-sized, glowing faintly blue beneath the crimson haze. A little girl in Victorian clothes, her face pale as chalk, ribbons trailing from her braids.

She looked at me like she recognized me. Then she opened her hand. A coin rested on her palm—silver fused with black stone, etched with runes. "Reaper," she whispered, voice thin and crackling, as if it came from inside a broken radio. "He's taking names."

My breath hitched. "Whose names?"

"All of them." Her eyes flicked past me, toward the fog. "He eats them so no one remembers who they were."

The words made my stomach knot. Names were powerful in this world and in ours. Erasing a name here could erase the person associated with it.

I crouched, slowly reaching for the coin. "What's your name, sweetheart?"

She tilted her head. "I had one."

Then her form trembled, edges fraying. Her hand dropped the coin into the mud before she dissolved like ash in the wind.

Ghost whimpered.

I went to pick up the coin, but Death kicked it away. "Just like the water, it's a trap."

The whispering around us swelled—hundreds of voices rising and falling in a broken chant.

You must pay... You must pay...

A chill ran down my spine. The clock was still ticking. I held Ghost close and twirled the scythe in my hand.

"We've got to go," Death said. "Time's up."

The bond heated inside my chest. I ignored the voices, focusing on it, fanning its nonexistent flames. "Not yet." I spun in a circle. "We're close. The connection is stronger."

Before he could respond, the scythe vibrated sharply, blade flaring white. The light cut through the fog like a flare gun. Ahead, a structure rose out of the red haze—a massive obelisk of fused bone and shadow, taller than a cathedral.

"Anchor Point Two," Death said. His voice was low and... reverent? Or was that simply a cover for something else, like fear?

The obelisk pulsed—steady, rhythmic, like a heartbeat.

The same heartbeat I felt through the bond.

Killion's.

The obelisk towered over us, half-buried in the shifting fog, ribs of bone latticed with veins of molten shadow. Every few seconds, it pulsed—slow, steady, alive.

The scythe quivered. The light from its blade fought

with the obelisk's red glow, and the air between the two shimmered like a storm front waiting to break.

Ghost struggled to get down. She could sense it too—the power bleeding out of this thing. I set her on her feet. "Stay close."

Death's gaze raked the structure. "He's turned a Sanctum into a siphon. Every lost soul that touches this anchor is drained—memory, essence, everything. It feeds directly into the Ferryman's gate."

"So how do we stop it?" I asked, tightening my grip on the scythe.

He gave me a sharp look. "Carefully."

"Not exactly reassuring."

A humorless twitch ghosted across his mouth. "You're not easily reassured."

I stepped closer, the scythe leading me like a compass needle fixed on disaster. The closer I came, the heavier the pull. My tattoo seared. "It's tugging on me."

Death's tone hardened. "It's tugging on Killion."

He was right. I could feel the soul bond fluttering erratically in my chest, like Killion was pounding on the inside of my ribs, trying to be heard. His fear mixed with fury—then flickered out.

The obelisk's surface rippled. Shadows peeled away like skin. Beneath them, I saw reflections—hundreds of faces screaming silently, eyes glowing silver. Every one of them was trapped.

At the center of the reflections, one face moved.

My pulse stopped.

Killion.

His reflection stared up at me through the bone-glass surface, lips forming my name. His hand lifted, pressing against the inside of the obelisk.

I stepped forward instinctively.

Death's hand shot out, catching my arm. "Don't touch it!"

The reflection flickered, twisting into something monstrous—his features melting into black water. A grin split the darkness, stretching too wide.

The Ferryman's voice slithered through the air. *"Break the seal, Reaper, and I'll let you keep what's left of him."*

"Not a chance," I said, but my voice came out thinner than I wanted.

Death's weapon flared, the curved blade hissing. "Strike on my mark. If we sever the connection at the wrong point, you'll be dragged in with him."

"How do I know the right point?"

He glanced at me, the faintest smirk twisting his mouth. "The scythe knows."

"I'm trusting this to a blade that's been rejecting me?" I asked. "Doesn't seem like the best plan."

The scythe burned hot in my hand. The hum became a scream. *Kill!*

I raised it. Death mirrored me.

"Now!" he shouted.

Our blades came down together.

The obelisk split open with a thundering sound. Red fire erupted from the crack, spiraling upward in a column that tore through the matching sky. Souls poured out in streaks of silver and gold, racing away into the darkness.

Ghost barked once, triumphant, before collapsing at my feet.

"Killion!" I yelled into the light. "Come on, I can feel you! Come back!"

For a heartbeat, I thought it worked. A silhouette took shape in the fire—tall, broad-shouldered. His hand reached toward me—then the light imploded, sucking itself inward.

He was gone.

"No!" I shouted.

The obelisk shattered into a thousand bone fragments, raining down on us. I threw up a hand over my head, ducking.

The ground heaved, and Death grabbed my arm to steady me. "Anchor Two is severed. But he's still trapped."

I stared at the crater where the obelisk had stood. My teeth chattered, and my body shook. I blinked through the dust floating in the air, searching for the bond. It was there, faint again. "Then we find the next one."

Death's gaze bore into me, his fingers tightening on my biceps. "You can't save him, Chloe. I have to take you back."

I jerked from his grasp and nearly toppled. "I'm. Not. Leaving."

If he wanted to, he could simply blink and whisk me away. Instead, he held out a hand.

I shifted back. "Didn't you hear me?"

"Just take my hand. I'm not going to force you across the Veil. All I want to do is give you enough energy to make it to the next anchor."

On the horizon, more red flares bloomed in the fog. "How can I trust you?"

"There are at least three of them, and you and Ghost are out of time. Trusting me is your only choice."

Reluctantly, I stretched out my hand, hovered it over his. Our eyes locked, and for a second, I saw the being behind the facade he always leaned on. The being Grim Zero had once been bonded to, like Killion and I were now. Death had loved me in that lifetime, and it ate him up that in this incarnation, I loved the master vampire.

"I'm not leaving until I find him," I ground out.

He gripped my hand. "I know."

Grim Zero lunged to the surface, clinging to him. Energy surged from his palm into mine. My fingers clutched him of their own accord, and his power rushed up my arm and straight to my chest. Words I didn't understand came out of my mouth—a message from Grim Zero to him. They made no sense to me, but I saw the shock on his face, saw his eyes widen. For a single breath, my chest squeezed, locked in their connection. Unbidden memories swirled through my mind, and I felt it—a second soul bond thread going taut.

Music flooded my ears. Shivers rolled down my spine. The universe billowed out in front of me, endless. Timeless. A million lifetimes flickering into existence and winking out just as quickly. My eyes rolled up in my head, and I swayed.

He broke the connection, drawing his power back. I continued to stagger, my mouth dry and heart pounding. Grim Zero trembled inside me. The connection to Death's power might be broken, but her connection to him was back in play.

"I..." I rubbed my chest, peering at him. "I don't know what she just did."

He glanced away, pain and vulnerability on his face. "It's nothing."

But it was. Her grief swept through me. Her longing. If Oblivion wiped us all out, their love story would be erased as surely as mine and Killion's.

Ghost gave a faint growl. When I glanced at her, she lifted her head. I froze. "Uh, Death?"

He swung around at my tone.

I pointed. "I think we have another problem."

Her eyes, usually pale silver, now glowed blood-red.

SEVENTEEN

Ghost's eyes gleamed a deep, feral crimson that didn't belong to her, didn't belong, period.

"Ghost?" My voice cracked as I dropped beside her. Her small body trembled, and her lip curled back. The fur along her spine flickered, black smoke curling off her like ash from a dying fire. "Hey, sweetheart, look at me."

She lifted her head. For a heartbeat, I saw my reflection in her gaze—split down the middle. Half alive, half unmade. Then her pupils shrank, and she whimpered, pressing her head into my palm as if trying to hide.

Death knelt a few feet away, his expression unnerved. "She's absorbing the corruption."

"What?" A ringing started in my ears. "That's impossible." My voice wobbled. "She's a psychopomp. She's immune to everything."

He didn't blink. "Not everything."

A thought hit. "He's corrupting her like he did my scythe."

Death rose, staring at the shifting terrain. "Oblivion is corrupting the laws of death. Both the blade and the psychopomp are instruments of that."

Ghost whimpered again, her form flickering for a quick moment. I gathered her into my arms, ignoring the way her form buzzed against my skin like static. Her heartbeat fluttered under my hand. "You're not going anywhere," I whispered fiercely. "You hear me? You're mine. I won't let him have you."

Death loomed over us. "You can't save her here."

Ghost shifted in my arms—as if the Ghost Lands themselves were trying to pull her apart molecule by molecule. "Take her back. To the living world. Will that fix her?"

"I don't know." The honesty in his tone unnerved me. "But I'm not leaving you here. Either we all go, or we all move forward."

Before I could argue, Ghost wriggled free, dropping to the ground. Her head snapped toward our right, ears forward, body trembling. A growl built in her chest.

The scythe reacted, too, its blade angling in the same direction like a divining rod that had caught the scent of something unholy.

"Guess that's our answer," I muttered, gripping the trembling weapon tighter. "But I don't like it."

Ghost curled her lip again and jetted ahead of us. The fog grew thicker, pressing close, whispering against my skin. The red veins running through it were brighter now—no longer faint threads, but pulsing arteries that cast sickly light over the landscape.

The ground underfoot changed. Bone jutted up in broken arches, towering like the remains of a ruined cathedral. Silver dust clung to every surface, glowing as we passed. Each step reverberated loudly in my ears, as if the Ghost Lands themselves were an echo chamber.

A cold tremor rippled up my wrist and through my right arm. I stopped, scooting my jacket sleeve back. Vines of crimson light threaded under my flesh, both hot and cold.

"That can't be good," I said.

Death's eyes snapped to mine, then to my arm. "The corruption is spreading." His voice was clipped. "Through your bond with Ghost and the scythe. Possibly even through your bond with Killion. It's infecting you."

I flexed my hand, jaw tightening. I pushed against the creeping perverse energy, remembering all the lessons Killion had taught me about controlling my necromancy and how I had life-giving magic. It had been a while since I'd called on that power, but I did so now.

A wash of warm energy burst from my chest. The vines stopped mid-tangle. With a shaky breath, I smiled as I showed my arm to Death. "Looks like I can handle it."

He looked unconvinced. "If you stay here, it will worsen. The corruption feeds on connections." His gaze touched the blade and the dog. "You have too many."

Ghost had paused a few yards ahead. "Come," I called to her. Reluctantly, she returned, and I pushed the same necromantic magic into her. Her body flickered, then stabilized. "Thatta girl. Neither of us is going anywhere."

Death exhaled, long-suffering. "Foolish bravado," he muttered. "That's why the living break faster than the dead."

"Then I guess it's a good thing I'm somewhere in between."

We followed the pull of the blade, Ghost leading us. The red glow deepened ahead, pulsing like a dying star. The air thickened, heavy as thunderclouds before a storm.

The scythe's tug grew more insistent. I felt it before I heard it, a pulse that vibrated straight through the marrow of my bones. The fog thinned ahead, and a faint shimmer bled through it.

We stepped onto the bank of another river—narrower than the one that guarded the Sanctum, but just as maligned. Its surface glowed like molten glass, rippling with slow waves of silver fire.

What floated there took my breath away.

Names. Thousands of them. Each etched across the surface in feverish light—layered, overlapping, fading. Every few seconds, one of them flared into red and gold flames and then burned away, leaving nothing but smoke.

Cold teeth sank into my spine. "What is happening?"

Death crouched beside the bank, his coat brushing the ground. He watched as another name turned to flames and winked out. "These are the names of souls tethered between realms. He's obliterating them."

I stared at the glowing current as his words sank in,

my grip on the scythe so tight that my knuckles turned white. One name shone brighter than the rest, curling in elegant script. *Raphael Dupré.*

I knew that name. A vampire who tended Killion's wine collection. He'd brought us a bottle of sauvignon blanc the previous week, smiling shyly when I'd thanked him. "You mean like the Undead?" I asked.

The letters turned to flame and vanished.

Death's gaze traced the current, his jaw tight. "Undead magic is potent, and the easiest for him to gain control over. It's feeding him."

I sank to my knees, staring into the burning water. "If their names disappear here—"

"They're erased." He touched the edge of the current, just for a moment, and the current recoiled from him. "No trace they ever existed."

The realization hit like a punch to my chest. "He feeds on them as they feed on the living."

Death's expression darkened. "Yes. Every erasure gives him more power, but also more hunger. Like vampires crave blood, he craves power."

The scythe thrashed in my hand. Ghost growled with menace. The names began burning faster now, blinking out in bursts of light. "Does he know we're here?"

"That would be my guess. We did take out two anchors."

The fog curled close, tickling my ears, my neck. The river's glow dimmed, and for a moment, the Ghost Lands went still.

My chest warmed, and a spark pressed against my ribs. A whisper—muted, distorted, but unmistakable.

"Chloe…"

Killion.

The bond rocked me. "Did you hear that?"

Death stiffened, shaking his head. "What?"

"Killion is calling me."

"You're hearing voices."

Killion's magic prickled against my skin. "No. It's real. Killion's calling me."

"Or something wants you to think he is."

I turned, grasping onto the connection and letting it guide me. The fog parted, revealing a shallow crevice where light bled up from the ground.

Hundreds of orbs floated above the surface, glowing gold and blue. Each one rippled and whispered—voices, soft as breath, layered like the echo of a dream.

Ghost tucked her tail, laying her ears back. Death shifted behind me, his magic and voice filled with warning. "Chloe, don't—"

But I was already moving.

The air sizzled as I stepped closer. One of the orbs flared brighter than the rest, silver bleeding into its glow. It expanded, reshaping.

Killion stood there. Or something that looked like him—pale, beautiful, suffering. His eyes met mine, filled with the same defiance and love that had undone me a hundred times before.

"Chloe," he whispered, reaching out.

I reached back. "I'm here."

"Stop!" Death's voice cracked like thunder behind me.

Too late. My fingers brushed the light.

The orb exploded outward—and a thousand voices poured through me. They weren't whispers anymore. They were memories.

Names. Faces. Lives. All burning, twisting, collapsing. I saw a child laughing in sunlight, a soldier falling in mud, a woman burying her lover. I saw Killion—a hundred moments of him, from centuries I hadn't lived. Then they all screamed as one and broke apart.

Pain lanced through my skull. Blood poured from my nose. The world tilted. I clutched my head, choking on a scream of my own.

"Enough!" Death's voice cut through the chaos.

He was beside me in a blur, his weapon slicing through the air. Darkness folded around us, swallowing the light whole. The screams died. The orbs winked out, one by one.

Silence crashed back in. The stillness roared louder in my ears than the screams had. I collapsed to my knees, shaking, the scythe heavy in my hand. Blood dripped to the ground from my nose. I felt a warm trickle of it leaking from my left ear.

Death knelt beside me, his expression unreadable but softer than usual. "Are you all right?"

I wiped the blood from my top lip with the back of my hand. "No."

A hand landed on my shoulder. His magic skittered

along my neck, my skull. I didn't fight it. "What did you see?"

I stared at the hollow, the darkness still rippling, as if echoing with more souls trapped within. "Ghosts," I said, voice rough. My stomach heaved at the idea that Killion was now one of them. "Their memories."

Death's gaze flicked toward the empty air where the orbs had been. "A soul stripped of memory is just a shell. What did I tell you?"

I refused to believe Killion was dead—he couldn't be. I was still here. "It was an illusion, like you said." Only, it hadn't felt that way. "What if *all* of this is an illusion?"

Death cut his eyes to me.

I turned in a circle. "Killion always tells me to *question the premise* when I'm failing to fix a problem. If we're going off the wrong premise, no matter what we do to solve a problem, it won't work."

"We crossed the Veil, Chloe." He gestured at our surroundings. "We're in the Ghost Lands. They're real."

"But they're wrong, remember? Corrupted. We've stepped into a *version* of them."

His eyes narrowed on me. "What are you saying?"

"What if all of this is an illusion, even Killion's disappearance, so Oblivion and the Ferryman could get us to come here?"

His head snapped back, his skepticism morphing into comprehension. An ugly one at that. "Leaving Shepherd's Rest and the portals the Ferryman is using in Danté's Grove unattended."

Those icy teeth scraped down my spine. "We need to get back, right now," I said.

The scythe groaned. My tattoo seared hot. Ghost barked.

Death grunted, grabbed Ghost, and gestured for me to take his hand. I did, and I sucked in a breath, waiting to be transported home.

Only, nothing happened. There was no cartwheeling through space. We simply stood there, facing each other.

I blinked. "Well? Go ahead. We need to get back home."

He swore and ground his teeth together. "I'm trying."

His grip tightened on me. His power surged, making my bones ache. Ghost trembled in his arm.

I blinked again, understanding causing my stomach to pitch. "You can't transport us?"

His lips pressed into a hard line. He dropped his hand. Before he could answer, dozens of ghosts suddenly materialized in a circle around us.

We both automatically raised our weapons. Ghost launched from his hold. "Looks like we overstayed our welcome," he said.

EIGHTEEN

The ghosts closed in.

They weren't the gentle kind that whispered regrets or asked to be led home—these were echoes stripped of faces, their features melted into slick hollows of shadow and light.

They moved like smoke given hunger, their bodies flickering in and out as if memory itself were unraveling.

The scythe jerked violently in my hand, its edge flaring before dimming again. It wanted to reap—but there was nothing left of these ghosts. No souls, no essence, just fragments of thought and emotion— gnashing forms.

Death hissed, stepping in front of me. His weapon cut a black arc through the air, scattering the nearest specters. They didn't vanish. The air hissed where his blade passed, but the ashes of their forms reassembled midair.

He paused, his voice incredulous. "They've become self-sustaining."

"Like ghosts caught in a loop," I muttered, backing toward Ghost.

One drifted too close. Its hand stretched toward me and seared my skin—the same bone-deep cold as the Ferryman's river. My tattoo blazed again in warning. I swung the scythe.

The blade met no resistance, slicing through vapor and light. The ghost cried out. The pressure hit behind my eyes and shoved me back a step—but didn't dissipate. My nose started bleeding again. I wobbled on my feet.

"Reaping won't work," Death said. "They're beyond death."

"Then what are they?"

"What's left when Oblivion consumes a soul but doesn't finish the meal."

I screwed up my bleeding nose and used the hem of my shirt to staunch the flow. "So we're surrounded by leftovers?"

He shot me a look. "A macabre but accurate analogy."

The ghosts circled tighter, their movements synchronizing into a predatory rhythm. The air crackled with static and whispering voices. Ghost barked, her brave voice driving the faceless echoes back. They swirled in a slow retreat, a tide of shadows rippling.

The bond woke again, but felt as if it were buried deep under layers of ice.

My hand went to my chest. "Killion," I breathed. The bond flickered—a fragile thread, weak but alive.

"Don't," Death warned, already sensing the shift in my aura. "Not again. Whatever you feel, it's the Ferryman's illusion. You know it is."

The scythe disagreed. It yanked in my hand, the silver edge pointing left—toward the fog thickening into a deeper darkness. The ground trembled.

"Illusion or not," I said, steadying it, "I have to check."

I followed the pull, Ghost sticking close, her tail down but resolute. She sniffed the air. The shadows parted, revealing a wide, rectangular pit in the earth.

A grave. A massive one, at that. Even Death hesitated beside it.

It was filled with water. The liquid shifted and shimmered, reflecting warped images. The surface gurgled softly, as though the grave were breathing. A hundred faces rippled beneath it, blinking up and vanishing like reflections on broken glass. The smell was all river rot.

I knelt at the edge. The bond surged again, beating in sync with the ripples. "He's here," I whispered. "I can feel him."

Death's shadow loomed over me. "This is the Ferryman's work. A soul well. He's using it to collect what's left of the erased."

The water stirred. A shape moved in its depths—vague, humanoid. I leaned closer.

Killion's face surfaced for a split second, his lips forming my name. "Chloe!"

I gasped, reaching out—but Death's hand clamped on my arm. "Touch that water, and you won't come back."

The surface went still again, leaving only the reflection of a full moon above us.

My heart slammed in my chest. "If that's not him, why does the bond keep throbbing?"

"I don't know." Death pinched the bridge of his nose.

Killion surged again, breaking the surface. He was in vampire form, fangs descended, face furious. "Chloe!"

He stuck out a hand. I grabbed it.

His body was a dead weight. As he sank again, he pulled me headfirst into the grave.

I gasped, sucking in the frigid water. I coughed and flailed, Killion's hand slipping from my grasp.

Just as I was about to become fully submerged, Death grabbed the waistband of my pants and hauled me out.

I sputtered and smacked at him. My teeth chattered. "I had him!"

"Chloe." His voice was sharp, but behind the authority was something else—fear. "You dive into that, you may as well carve your own epitaph."

I wiped water from my eyes, my hand coming away bloody. The icy water had stopped my nose bleed, but there was still plenty on my hands and clothes. "At least I'll go out swinging."

Ghost whined and pawed at the edge of the pit, then glanced at me—as if to say *I'm going in*.

I grabbed her scruff. "I'm going with you."

Death swore softly, ancient and ugly. "You'll need an anchor."

"Are you volunteering?"

The bond tugged hard enough to steal my breath. The scythe followed, jerking me into the grave.

Cold hit first—liquid ice swallowing me whole. The scythe lit up, becoming a flashlight in the murk with a thin, trembling beam. A splash, and Ghost was with me. I gripped her fur again.

Shapes drifted below: fragments of bone, faces, half-formed bodies dissolving in the current.

Voices brushed my mind, soft and endless. The psychopomp and I kicked downward, chasing Killion. The deeper I swam, the brighter the scythe burned, pulling me faster until the dark turned red.

The bond kicked hard, and I saw him suspended in the current, arms outstretched, silver chains wound around his wrists. He was still in vampire form, his eyes open but empty, pupils blown wide. The Ferryman stood behind him, shadow-tall and faceless, one hand resting on Killion's shoulder.

"Let him go!" I shouted, though the water swallowed the words. The Ferryman turned his head slowly, the void of his face catching the scythe's light and swallowing it.

Reaper, his voice whispered directly into my skull. *Trade for trade. Debt for debt.*

Pain seared through my chest as the bond yanked tight, and Killion's gaze zeroed in on me. He shook his head violently.

Death's voice thundered through the current, distant but furious. "Chloe! Get out!"

But it was too late. The Ferryman's hand lifted, and

the chains around Killion blazed. The current grabbed me, dragging me down. The last thing I saw before the world went scarlet was Killion's eyes, bright with terror—and love.

Something slashed through the red—light, fast, and furious. A sound like a thousand wings tearing the air rippled through the water.

Ghost.

Her psychopomp form, all monster dog and spectral fur, eyes burning silver-blue, grabbed me and hauled me to Killion.

The Ferryman's faceless head snapped toward her as she hurtled past me, colliding with him in a burst of fire. His shroud tore apart like smoke in a hurricane, reforming instantly—but he staggered.

The scythe blazed white. The pulse of the bond roared through me. *Now.*

The chains around Killion's wrists shimmered with runes that looked half-script, half-vein, pumping darkness into him. He was fading, his skin gray, his eyes dull.

My lungs screamed for air. I didn't care.

I swung the scythe. The first strike hit like a stone, reverberating in my hand so hard that I nearly dropped the blade.

The next cracked one of the glowing links. Power surged up my arm, making my vision go white. I swung again, roaring through the water.

The Ferryman screeched—no sound, just pressure, a psychic roar that made the water quake. Ghost lunged again, her fangs closing on his arm, forcing him backward.

The chain on Killion's left wrist fractured under the scythe's next blow. I felt the bond flare—alive, furious, desperate.

He wrenched free, grabbed the last chain, and it shattered under his own strength. The light burst outward, a shockwave that sent the Ferryman tumbling into the dark.

My chest convulsed. My lungs burned, on fire. I clawed upward, dragging Killion with me. Ghost dove beneath and lifted us, her enormous body propelling us faster, the current churning around her.

The red faded to black, then to silver.

The surface shattered around us in a flash of silver light. Killion and Ghost burst through first, gasping, dragging me with them onto land. Ghost erupted with a howl that rolled across the Ghost Lands like thunder.

Death waited on the shore, coat whipping in an invisible wind. That's when I realized my blade had disappeared. "My scythe!" I shouted, lunging back toward the water.

"Move!" Death bellowed, motioning us to get away from the open, watery grave.

Behind us, the Ferryman's scream split the water—a guttural, endless wail. The ghosts answered, hundreds of them rising from the fog, faceless and hungry.

Death lifted his hand. For a heartbeat, I thought he meant to strike them. Instead, he pressed his palm to his chest. A black mist began to bleed out, a living shadow that writhed and coiled like a serpent. The mist hissed where it hit the air, eating the light around him. His jaw clenched.

"Death—what are you—?"

"Opening a door," he gritted out. "And paying the toll."

The shadows peeled outward, slicing the air like tearing fabric. The space in front of us cracked open— light and darkness swirling together, forming a jagged wound in the world. A violent force jerked on me.

"Go!" he shouted.

Ghost lunged through first, her glow streaking into the void. Killion hissed through his fangs, and I hooked my arm under his. He coughed, blood mixing with river water. "Chloe—"

"Not now." I dragged him toward the portal as the first of the ghosts reached the bank. Their hands clawed the air, leaving trails of red fire in their wake. My lungs burned, my muscles screamed, but the thought of losing him again propelled me on.

Death's essence bled faster, the mist curling from his chest like smoke from a dying flame. The wound in the Veil shrank around its edges, already fighting to close. "Now, Grave Girl!"

I tightened my grip on Killion's hand, met Death's burning eyes for half a second, and jumped.

The cold vanished. The screams vanished. Gravity grabbed me and slammed me home.

We hit hard—on grass, not mud—and rolled down a short slope until we landed at the base of a headstone. I lay there, sucking in air that tasted like rain and dirt and life. The sound of breathing—real breathing—was the sweetest thing I'd ever heard.

Killion groaned beside me. Ghost shook herself, scattering water beads across the ground.

I pushed up on one elbow, wheezing, but so happy to see Killion, I threw my arms around him.

His arms locked around me, solid and trembling, and for one impossible heartbeat, the world stopped spinning. The bond hummed with relief.

Death stumbled through after us, his coat shredded, the hole in his chest already sealing itself. He straightened slowly, eyes flicking upward.

Above us, the sky was no longer red—it was deep indigo, split by streaks of moonlight so bright they looked like blades. Clouds whipped fast across the heavens.

The moon hung massive and swollen, its light stark and unnatural. A perfect ring of shadow circled it, glowing faintly crimson.

"The Grave Moon," I whispered.

Death nodded once, grim. "We're too late."

NINETEEN

I rolled onto my back, lungs burning, and stared straight up at the sky.

Peeking through heavy clouds, the moon loomed huge and heavy above the cemetery—full, blood-bright, and wrong. The eerie ghost halo circling it cast the headstones in shades of violet and black.

"It wasn't full when we left," I insisted.

Death straightened, still grasping at his chest. "There's no real time in the Ghost Lands. The Ferryman didn't only distract us, he stalled us so he could do...this." His hands motioned at the graveyard.

A scream tore across the rolling hill of Shepherd's Rest, high and ragged. I pushed up to my knees in time to see Aurora in a casting circle. Her arms were out, her head thrown back, her mouth calling out a spell.

The circle glowed with her power and that of the words she chanted. Andy held a silver-bladed staff as a horde circled them. Harlow and Katarina were on top of two of the highest crypts, calling out orders to vampires stationed throughout the place.

Killion groaned beside me, one hand braced in the dirt. His aura flickered in jagged bursts—light leaking through cracks that spidered down his neck and chest. His voice was shredded velvet. "I hate portals," he rasped.

I glanced at Death, who was supporting himself with his hands on his knees. My own energy was flagging after so much time in the Ghost Lands and all we'd survived. Digging for what I had left, I hauled Killion upright. His weight sagged against me. He was human-looking again, only his fangs still on display to give him away. "You're burned out. You need to stand down and let the rest of us handle this."

The corner of his mouth twitched. "Not likely."

"Don't argue." I forced him to a concrete bench. An angel statue wept near it. Ghost followed close on our heels, and I pointed at her. "Guard him."

Death drew his weapon, scanning the area like a general assessing his last stand. His voice carried like thunder over the dead as he addressed everyone. "The Grave Moon amplifies everything. We're out of time. We make our stand here, now."

Killion's aura dimmed again. I brushed my fingers over his jaw, wishing I could keep him out of this just once. "Don't move," I whispered.

He caught my wrist, his eyes briefly clearing. "You're as drained as I am. I can feel it."

"You need blood, and I need one of Pennyworth's feasts, but—"

"Master!" The butler appeared, racing over the ground toward us in his dress shoes and a neat wool coat. He handed Killion a thermos. "Here."

Killion and I exchanged a wry smile. "Your timing is perfect," my husband said.

Pennyworth straightened, beaming. "And for you, Mistress." He handed me a protein bar—chocolate caramel—and a sword.

"Fantastic," I said, even as Death strode up and snagged the bar from my hand. "Hey!"

Pennyworth produced another and peeled the wrapper for me. "I never come to a fight empty-handed."

"Stay with your vamps, Fangboy," Death ordered, pointing in Katarina's direction before finishing the bar in two bites. "I'll take Grave Girl." He tossed the wrapper to the ground. Pennyworth hurriedly picked it up and shoved it in a pocket.

Killion pulled me in and kissed me. For one impossible heartbeat, the war fell away. "Come back to me," he said, grazing my bottom lip with his fangs.

My throat tightened. I gave him a squeeze. "That's the plan."

Aurora's circle flared a dazzling bright white, but then shattered, rocking the night.

I sucked in a breath, ready to rush toward her as ghosts poured through the broken wards, hundreds of them—sickly red instead of white, their forms bending like melted wax.

Then the mist cleared, and I pulled up short. At the

center of the circle stood the Ferryman, a river of red running past his feet.

Ghost growled, hackles up. Death's shadow merged with mine. "Ready?" he asked.

No time to eat. I gave a nod and stuffed the bar in my pocket, gripping the sword with both hands. "Always."

We charged.

The ground trembled as we closed the distance to the Ferryman. The world bent around him like a heat mirage. His faceless head turned toward us, and the river at his feet hissed like acid on stone.

"Careful," Death warned, his voice cutting through the din. "He's not alone."

Shapes crawled out of the shadows—massive, skeletal forms dragging themselves from the broken graves. Bone and shadow fused into armor, eyes burning with red light. Sentinels.

Their presence made the air vibrate, a droning buzz that pressed against my skull. The first one unfurled fully —taller than a mausoleum, its ribcage carved with runes that glowed. The second followed, carrying a weapon that looked like a halberd made of human spines.

"Remind me to thank SMG for leaving the door unlocked," I muttered, twirling the sword in my grip.

Death cracked a grim smile. "You distract them. I'll carve a path."

"Distract them? Sure. I'll just wave my shiny blade and hope they're into that."

"Chloe—"

"Yeah, yeah, I'm going!"

The first Sentinel lunged. The ground caved under its weight, sending splinters of marble and bone flying. I dove left, rolling behind a cracked angel statue as its halberd slammed down, missing me by inches. The impact cratered the earth, and a wave of cold wind blasted outward, carrying the stench of decay.

I sprang up and slashed at its leg. The sword connected, and bone splintered, shrieking. Souls poured from the wound—dozens of them—screaming as they fled upward in ribbons of light.

The Sentinel staggered, but didn't fall. Its fist swung out, catching me in the jaw and sending me flying. I hit a headstone hard enough to rattle my teeth. The concrete didn't even bust.

"Ten out of ten," I gasped. "Sturdy craftsmanship."

"Try this."

I glanced up to see Mei Han—not a hologram, but in the flesh. She wore her usual prim suit and air of authority, even though she was no longer in charge of SMG. She held out my scythe. "You can't win against the Ferryman with anything less."

I snatched my blade from her hand, feeling its hilt warm in my palm. "What are you doing here?"

"Correcting a wrong." She tugged on the hem of her jacket and glanced around. "That belongs to you, not SMG. They shouldn't have taken it. Again."

"You stole it?"

Her lips pressed into an unforgiving line. "Believe it or not, I wish to see this world survive, just like you do."

Before I could say anything else, she vanished.

I smiled as I twirled the blade. "Will wonders never cease?"

"Less yapping!" Death blurred past me, his weapon slicing through the second Sentinel's midsection. His shadows coiled and struck, wrapping the creature like barbed chains. Thunder echoed with every impact. "More killing!"

Kill, the scythe echoed.

But Death's Sentinel wasn't dead. The wound I'd given mine had only slowed him down. They both reformed right before our eyes.

"Cut them down, and they come back?" I whined. "That's cheating!"

"Life's not fair," Death grunted, readying his weapon again.

The first Sentinel bellowed, a shockwave that shattered the nearest crypt. Ghost barreled out of the fog in full psychopomp fury. The Sentinel reeled backward, shrieking as she tore into it.

"She's supposed to be guarding Killion." My balance was wobbly. The world spun. "But thank you," I called to her.

A third Sentinel rose behind Death. "Behind you!" I yelled.

He spun, but too late—the creature's halberd slammed into his side. He went flying, black mist spilling from the wound as he crashed into a marble monument.

"Death!"

He lifted his head, teeth bared. "Still here."

Here, but as wounded and drained as I was. I glanced

back at where I'd left my soulmate, but he wasn't there. Fear pinched my heart, and I started to run to the spot, cursing Ghost for leaving his side, when I saw him. He and Harlow were fighting a pack of ghosts near a new circle Aurora was setting down.

Aurora stood in the center of the cemetery again, her hair plastered to her cheeks, chalk-white from exhaustion. The remnants of her circle sparked and hissed beneath her boots. She was trying to re-draw the sigils—bare hands scraping symbols into the dirt, raw power bleeding from her palms.

Andy stood guard in front of her, his staff a blur as he kept the ghosts at bay. "Keep them back!" he shouted.

The scythe gyrated violently in my hands, alive and furious. I helped Death to his feet. "None of us will be still here for long if we don't end this."

I sprinted forward, drawing on everything I had left. The blade cut arcs through the night, every swing brighter, faster. Ghost finished ripping her Sentinel apart. Death unleashed himself on another. The three of us drove through them, carving a path to the Ferryman.

The last Sentinel blocked my way, its face splitting into dozens of screaming mouths. I planted my feet, the bond with Killion throbbing in my chest. He was faltering. So was I.

"I'm not dead yet," I snarled and swung.

The scythe hit the creature square in the chest. A flare of silver burst outward, so bright it turned night to day. The thing shrieked, imploded, and vanished—taking its brethren with it.

When the light faded, the graveyard was eerily quiet again—except for the hiss of the Ferryman's river.

He stood untouched, watching us—*me*. As the clouds shifted, a face appeared under the hood. His soulless eyes were pools of silver water, swirling. They met mine, then dropped to the scythe.

"Don't let him confuse you with illusions," Death murmured for my ears only. "Remember what he can do."

The river behind the Ferryman widened, its current curling through the graves like tiny rivers.

The Ferryman's voice slid into my mind like an echo of water under stone. *Reaper. You've fought well. But you've always misunderstood me.*

I tightened my grip on the scythe, sweat trickling down the back of my neck. "You want to finish what Oblivion started."

No.

That single word hung between us. The moonlight flared, staining the fog blood-red.

Death flicked his eyes to me. "Don't let him in your head, Grave Girl."

"Too late," I muttered.

Oblivion devours and forgets, the Ferryman continued. *I remember. I collect. The Veil is broken. Your world is, too. But I will remake it. You and I will bring a new world into being.*

Death grabbed my shoulder and shook me. "What is he saying?"

I repeated the Ferryman's words.

Death's voice cut through the wind, sharp and furious. "You were made to ferry the lost, not rule the living!"

The Ferryman's laughter echoed off the graves. "And you were made to end them. How's that balance working for you, old god?"

Death drew himself up. "Old god?"

I punched his bicep. "He's not wrong, although I wouldn't say you're a god exactly."

Andy drove his staff into the ground, shouting, "Aurora, now!"

Her circle flared to life again, white fire chasing through the lines she'd drawn. Runes spiraled outward in concentric rings, weaving through the cemetery like veins of light. Every stream of the soul river they met, steam rose.

The Ferryman's head turned toward her. "A witch forging a seal of her own. How quaint. Shall I show you what true rebirth looks like?"

He spread his hands. The river boiled, and from its surface rose a dozen more Sentinels. They fanned out, sprinting toward Aurora's circle.

"Go!" Death barked. He plunged into the fray, shadow-laced blade meeting the first Sentinel mid-charge.

I swung my scythe and felt it catch on something more solid than before—these creatures were merging flesh and spirit. Every hit tore away light and sinew. And still, they just kept coming.

Aurora's chant grew louder. The sigils brightened, feeding on the Grave Moon's power. The air sizzled.

"Hold them!" she shouted. "If the circle breaks again, we lose the seal entirely!"

The Ferryman's voice cut through everything. "Why fight for balance when you could wield eternity, Reaper? The scythe already answers to you. All that remains is to choose the hand it serves."

My blade shook, the blade flickering between silver and crimson. My tattoo burned white-hot, searing through my shirt.

Death roared across the chaos, "Don't listen to him!"

He fears what comes next, the Ferryman whispered in my head, his tone almost tender. *Oblivion will consume him, too. I am his deliverance. When I finish rewriting the world, even he will kneel.*

The words dropped like a hammer. Aurora's circle flared higher, her fire locking around the Ferryman—but he didn't retreat. He just watched me, as if waiting.

The scythe bucked and jerked. Ghost barked. The river at the Ferryman's feet surged, red light spearing toward the moon like a signal flare.

Death cursed under his breath. "He's merging his power with the Grave Moon!"

"And rewriting everything," I whispered.

The ground split open under my boots. The Ferryman's faceless head tilted once—mocking, knowing—and then he unleashed everything on us.

TWENTY

Graves split open in every direction. The red mist engulfed us, along with the echoing wails of the dead. The sky churned above us, clouds causing the Grave Moon to glow like a bloody lantern behind glass.

Aurora stood in the middle of the cemetery, her casting circle of salt and herbs scattering with an unseen wind. She knelt in the dirt, smearing ash and chalk with her bare hands, trying to redraw sigils that refused to stay whole. Her magic sparked wild, white-gold threads unraveling as fast as she could weave them.

"Hold it together, witch!" Death barked, his voice cutting through the chaos. He moved within a few feet from her, his shadows shielding her from the onslaught of ghosts pouring in through the broken wards.

"I *am* holding it!" she shouted back, hair whipping across her face. Her voice shook with fury and fear in equal measure. "He's eating the lines faster than I can remake them!"

The Ferryman's river had widened again. The water wasn't water anymore—it was soul stuff, thick and luminous, dragging pieces of the Veil itself into the mortal world. Every pulse sent ripples through the ground, making my bones ache.

The scythe heated against my palm, jerking with desperate, erratic movements. I forced my breath steady and focused on keeping it under control. If I let it slip, even once, it might decide I was the enemy.

"Killion, stay behind the line!" I shouted.

He ignored me, of course, sword in hand, face pale and drawn. Ghost had returned to him to guard his flank, her psychopomp form still holding but flickering around the edges.

"Grave Girl," Death said tightly, not looking away from the Ferryman's expanding shadow. "You're our best defense. Whatever you do, don't let go of that scythe."

The moon's light bent and fractured, spilling crimson reflections across my blade. The vampire troops were falling where they stood. I needed to do something, and I needed to do it fast.

"Hey, ugly," I called. I sliced the scythe through the air dramatically. "It's time you and I had a heart-to-heart."

The Ferryman stood as still as one of the statues, half corporeal, half liquid darkness. He extended a skeletal hand. Rivers of red and black licked across his fingers. His voice hit like a tremor. The words rattled through my chest. "Why fight what's already inevitable? I offer permanence."

Death snarled, his blade igniting with shadow fire. "You offer damnation."

The Ferryman lifted both arms. The soul river surged, overtaking half the cemetery. It ran into the open graves, rushing towards Aurora's circle. The ground beneath my feet shook, and for one breathless instant, the entire world seemed to tilt sideways.

I fell. The scythe went flying through the air.

And landed in the Ferryman's outstretched hand.

"Chloe!" Killion yelled through the air and through our bond.

"I'm...fine," I said, although I wasn't. My limbs shook, my vision swam. Water surged around me, getting in my mouth, my ears, my eyes.

Coughing and sputtering, I tried to raise my head up. Crawl. Anything.

The ground went out under me. I sank into a river of rot.

And then, a powerful force lifted me from the deluge. *Killion.*

The force of his magic plucked me out of the water. It sputtered, his energy too drained to sustain it. I landed hard on solid ground.

The glowing, pulsing moon shed a spotlight on me. The dead grass had a red tinge. The closest headstones glowed a sickly orange.

My stomach lurched, bringing up water. My head pounded. Shaking, I tried to rise on all fours, but my arms trembled so hard, they wouldn't hold me. A shadow cut off the light. Death and Killion both roared my name behind me. "Look out!" Katarina cried.

A glance over my shoulder showed me the Ferryman looming up behind me. He lifted the scythe high. "Time to pay the price of passage," he said.

Caleb's picture flashed through my mind. I huffed, drawing on Grim Zero's magic. Her anger. Her desire to be freed from my restraints.

"The First Blade is mine," she snarled from between my lips.

In a flash, the scythe descended, but I was too fast for it. I rolled to the left and felt her magic blast through me. I came to my feet without a thought, my hand shooting out.

The scythe changed direction mid-course. The hilt slammed into my palm, and the blade lit up with a silver fire. "*Kill*," it whispered in my mind.

"Kill," I echoed.

The Ferryman flinched back. I advanced. Death and Killion raced through the flooded cemetery to flank me, the three of us bearing down on the Ferryman.

Aurora screamed. Her circle surged, pushing the river back. She looked over her shoulder, eyes wild. "Whatever you're going to do—do it now!"

I slammed the scythe's end into the dirt and poured what magic I had left into the blade. The metal blazed, cutting a line through the red. Death joined me, his shadows twisting into the glow, reinforcing it. Killion did the same, Katarina adding her own blade to the mix.

Together, we forged a jagged, trembling barrier around Aurora's circle.

For a heartbeat, it held.

Then the Ferryman smiled—or at least, the shape of his face rippled with the suggestion of it. "You fight with borrowed power, Reaper." His gaze slid to Death. "And yours was never meant to last."

Mimicking me, he drove an oar tip into the ground, mocking us.

A shockwave hit, causing a mini-earthquake. Appearing at the Ferryman's side, Carmen looked like a zombie, her eye sockets hollow, her skin gray. She raised both hands and began murmuring.

The barrier shattered, the circle flickered, and Andy —who'd been driving ghosts back from Aurora's flank— screamed.

He fell to the ground hard. The sound made my heart stop.

Aurora cried his name, but her voice broke in half. The shockwave from the Ferryman's strike shredded the glowing sigils she'd redrawn. As Carmen continued to chant, lines of light snapped apart like live wires, their energy lashing out and scattering ghosts in white-hot bursts.

Killion moved before I did—a fast, sleek predator. He was at Andy's side in seconds, one hand gripping his shoulder, the other flashing with defensive magic that fizzled weakly around them both.

"Stay back!" Aurora shouted, struggling to reform the

circle. Her hands were shaking too hard to draw steady lines. "The power's volatile—"

Carmen yelled something in Latin. Andy's body arched off the ground, his back bowing, mouth open in a raw, soundless cry. The air around him pulsed with wild energy—streaks of red, silver, and black twisting together.

Ghost barked and lunged forward, planting herself between the Ferryman and me. I could taste metal on my tongue, and my gasping breaths came out in white plumes.

Killion gritted his teeth, trying to drag Andy backward. "He's burning up," he shouted. "It's the Ferryman's magic—he's trying to rip him apart!"

"No," Death said grimly, his blade raised again. "He's trying to remake him."

The Ferryman tilted his head toward us, voice silky with an acidic edge. "The wolf was stripped of his purpose. I'm merely giving him a new one."

A wave of heat and power burst outward. Killion was thrown back into a headstone, the stone cracking beneath him. He groaned, one arm clutching his side, blood staining his shirt.

"Killion!" I grabbed the scythe and sprinted to him, every instinct torn between defending him and reaching Andy.

"Go," he rasped, eyes flashing with faint red light. "I'll live."

"Not if you keep playing hero." I braced him upright just as Aurora stood, fierce and angry, and sent a wave of magic straight at Carmen.

The witches squared off, their magics colliding in a deafening *boom*.

Aurora gritted her teeth, her eyes flaring bright blue—the color of her panther form. Her arms shook, trying to keep Carmen's magic from reaching us. "I can't...stop...it!"

Andy's entire body blazed white. The veins in his neck shone silver; his heartbeat thundered so loud I felt it echo in my bones.

The Ferryman's shadow expanded, reaching for him. "He's mine," he hissed.

Killion pushed off the headstone, staggering toward him. "Over my Undead body."

He raised his hand, and scales emerged on his skin. I felt the call of his dragon power building. What was he doing? He was too weak to wield it.

But maybe not if I helped.

I dove beside Andy, my fingers gripping his wrist. His skin was frosty cold. I could feel the Ferryman's corruption writhing inside him—and something else pushing back. Using the bond, I channeled my own bit of dragon fire into Killion, giving his essence a boost.

Aurora fell to her knees on the other side of Andy, gripping his hand. "Come on," she whispered fiercely. "You've survived worse. You're not dying like this."

His eyes snapped open. In them, I saw his wolf reflected there. His body jerked. He let out a low, ragged growl. "I won't let him have me."

His back arched again—this time not in pain, but in

release. The magic around him detonated outward, knocking Aurora and me back.

I felt it before I saw it. Killion's dragon magic slammed into the Ferryman, and Andy's body quaked.

The wolf was waking up.

For a heartbeat, there was no sound—only a flash and the flood.

Andy screamed again, the sound splitting into a growl halfway through. His body twisted, bones cracking, reforming. His skin rippled with bands of light that crawled like molten silver through his veins.

Aurora reached for him, terrified. Tears streaked her ash-stained face. "No," she cried. "No, don't die—"

Death caught her arm, dragging her back just as a shockwave of Killion's power blasted the Ferryman and Carmen again. "Stay behind me," he ordered. "He's not dying."

I shielded my face from the radiance of Killion's magic, the air vibrating with a sound between a snarl and a storm. Fire singed everything in sight.

And then Andy's wolf emerged.

He burst free in a blaze of light and motion, fur gleaming white with silver streaking through it. He hit the ground hard, shoulders massive, eyes glowing the same crimson as the Grave Moon. Power rolled off him in waves, distorting the air, rattling the iron fences and crypt doors.

The bond faltered. I snapped my gaze to Killion. His arms trembled as he tried to hold them up. He gritted his teeth. Harlow and Katarina barked orders at the few remaining vampires, both of them moving toward their master, as if to help him.

Aurora gasped, her voice breaking into laughter and sobs. "By the cauldron..."

Ghost, still glowing faintly blue, gave a low, approving growl.

Andy raised his head and howled.

The sound tore straight through me. It hit every nerve, every thread of magic, every beat of my heart. The ghosts froze mid-attack, their twisted forms flickering as the sound rippled across the cemetery.

Aurora scrambled to her feet, spinning back toward her ruined circle. "That's it!" she cried, voice wild with realization. "His magic—it's stabilizing my spell! Killion's, too!"

"How?" I asked.

"He's grounding it!" she shouted. "Like a conduit between worlds—life, death, the Veil—it's all connected through them now!"

The Ferryman staggered, his shadow form warping. The red river around him recoiled, shrinking away from the light. "No!" he roared, the word vibrating the very ground. "You were mine!"

Andy lunged.

His claws hit the ground like blades. In a blur of fur and fury, he collided with the Ferryman, tearing through his cloak of shadows. The sound was part snarl, part scream, part thunder. The two forces clashed—corruption against rebirth, death against defiance.

Killion's body gave out. He slumped to the ground. I

stumbled to him, Katarina and Harlow holding the line to protect him.

"Is Andy...?" he asked, blinking in confusion.

"A wolf, yes." I hugged him to me. "And he's pissed."

Aurora's hands flew through a sigil pattern in the air, sealing the circle once more. The light of the Grave Moon reflected in her eyes as she spoke words older than time. The reformed barrier not only reformed, but it also shoved the waters back.

The Ferryman shrieked, reeling under the wolf's assault. His form flickered, leaking tendrils of red smoke that hissed where they hit the ground. He snatched up the oar and pummeled Andy with it.

Andy took the blow and sank into a crouch, his fur matted where the corruption tried to cling. His gaze cut to me, wild but lucid, and for the first time since Death, Killion, Ghost, and I had landed here, I felt hope.

"You wanted me and the blade," I yelled at the Ferryman, raising my scythe. "You got all of us instead."

The Ferryman straightened, the remains of his cloak snapping in the wind. "Then you'll fall together."

"Unlikely," Death murmured, stepping up beside me. Shadows coiled around him, solidifying into armor.

Killion moved to my other side, his fangs glinting. I don't know how he had the strength, but he was steady as he gripped my free hand and squeezed. Ghost padded forward, her head brushing against Andy's flank.

The five of us stood in a loose circle of power—life, death, undeath, spirit, and rebirth—all beating in sync with the Grave Moon.

TWENTY-ONE

The air went nuclear. A storm of energy and magic ripped through the cemetery.

The Ferryman stood, tattered and towering, dripping with power that ate the light around him. But he was wounded. Carmen crumpled at his feet, useless.

The Veil pulsed overhead, bleeding crimson light down onto the Ferryman as his river writhed upward, binding itself to the tear in the sky. The Grave Moon howled with it, wind shrieking through broken trees and cracked marble angels.

"Chloe!" Aurora's voice cut through the chaos. "He's drawing everything through you—the scythe, the circle, even *me*!"

I could barely hear her. My pulse roared in my ears, too fast. The scythe's silver blade threw off sparks of raw energy. Every heartbeat pulled more power through me until my vision blurred.

"Hold the wards!" Aurora shouted, voice hoarse, hair

plastered to her face with sweat and blood. Her hands trembled, but her voice didn't falter as she began a new chant.

Death raised his blade, voice ringing out like a death knell. "Let's do this!"

I charged forward, scythe blazing white, the air crackling as the blade drank in the moonlight. The Ferryman turned toward me, his hollow gaze shimmering with fury. "Reaper," he hissed, his voice a wound in my mind. "You were meant to serve me."

"Yeah, no," I said, spinning the scythe. "No one is going to serve you on my watch."

The blade sliced his form with a streak of silver-white light. The impact reverberated through my bones, every nerve screaming. He staggered, his shape distorting as shadows peeled away to reveal a glimpse of what was left beneath: bone, light, memory.

Killion joined me, raising his sword. "You have to stop channeling Grim Zero's magic!" he shouted over the roar. "It's killing you!"

I gasped, trying to hold the scythe steady. "If I stop, the Veil collapses."

"She's right," Death said. "If she shuts down Grim Zero, the entire realm collapses into the rift."

Above us, it shuddered wider, a mouth ready to devour all. The Ferryman threw his head back, laughter rolling like thunder. "You see, Reaper? Only I can save you from Oblivion."

The river surged, striking the ground in a spray of

spectral water. The nearest gravestones melted into liquid shadow.

Andy leapt, sinking his teeth into one of the red tendrils rising from the river, tearing it apart. Ghost dove beside him, her silver light interweaving with his, two primal forces colliding against the corruption.

For a heartbeat, the Ferryman faltered. His red glow flickered. The Veil's rip stuttered—just enough for me to breathe.

Killion grabbed my wrist, forcing my gaze to his. His eyes burned bright blue, the color of his dragon flame. "You're not alone. Take what you need."

The bond flared open between us—raw, infinite. His power flooded through me, cold as moonlight, fierce as wildfire. My veins turned incandescent.

The scythe blazed white. The light reached for the Grave Moon, wrapping around its light in silver ribbons that cut through the red. The entire sky shook.

Death shouted over the rising roar. "You're merging life and death—do you even know what that means?"

"Yes," I panted. "It means he doesn't get to win."

The Ferryman struck again, his oar-blades crossing, forming a spear of black light. He hurled it straight at me and shrieked, "You are *mine!*"

Killion jerked me sideways. The blast missed us by inches, obliterating an angel statue. The explosion scattered stones through the air.

The scythe split into dozens of arcs of energy. It became a conduit, its glow spreading into every living and unliving thing around us—the rift, even the moon.

Andy howled again. The sound harmonized with Ghost's shriek and Aurora's chanting, all of it feeding into Grim Zero's power.

For one breathtaking instant, the barrier between worlds sang.

The Ferryman reeled, his power fracturing.

"Hold on, Chloe!" Death shouted. "Keep the balance. You can do it!"

I wasn't sure I could. My body felt hollow, bones lit from within. Every nerve burned. I met the Ferryman's shadowed gaze. "I'm not yours, and I never will be."

I lifted the scythe higher.

The river convulsed upward again, coiling toward the Veil. Energy poured out of me in white-hot ribbons.

But it wasn't enough.

Killion dropped to one knee, clutching his chest. "Chloe, you're...fading."

And so was he. "I can handle it," I lied. The edges of my vision were fraying, my pulse scattering into static. "Just—keep the ghosts back!"

He nodded once, fangs bared, and launched himself toward a cluster of twisted spirits clawing their way out of the broken graves.

Aurora's voice cracked as it rose with her chanting. Andy's wolf form shuddered through another wave of corruption, his claws digging deep into the ground. Ghost whimpered and glanced back at me. I didn't know what to do.

The Ferryman stepped over Carmen's body. He

raised one skeletal hand, palm outward, and the world stopped.

The wind died. The magic in the air froze. The noises of fighting, of ghosts moaning...all of it ceased.

Then a spear of black light appeared in his grasp, and he thrust it straight at me.

I moved too slowly. The impact hit like being punched through time, cold and absolute. The spear didn't pierce flesh—it went through my soul.

For a heartbeat, I couldn't breathe. The scythe slipped from my fingers.

I heard Killion shout my name. Andy's growl broke into a howl of fury. But the pain held me fast, burning through every bond, every cell.

Then Death was there.

He caught me as I fell, one arm banded around my waist. Power flooded from him—black and endless—rushing into me like a tide.

"What—" I gasped, "are you doing?"

"Being the hero," he said, voice raw. He tore the spear from my chest. "I can't let you die. Not this time."

His essence poured into me, cold and infinite, filling every hollow place the Ferryman's weapon had left.

The ground cracked beneath us. The scythe leapt back into my hand, its blade now burning black and white at once.

Death wobbled. His voice was a whisper against my ear. "Finish it, Grave Girl."

The scythe's power ignited, laced with everything I was—Grim Zero, necromancer, vampire...dragon. Death.

I swung the blade up and pointed the top toward the hole in the Veil.

The light speared through the tear. The rip convulsed. The entire world tilted. The red river writhed and began to collapse inward, dragging the ghosts with it.

The Ferryman clawed toward me, voice breaking into static. "You can't kill what's eternal!"

Death appeared behind him in a blur, striking him down. His weapon sank deep into the Ferryman's spine, pinning him in place. The Ferryman bled white, pure soul-energy spilling out like burning water.

"Chloe!" Aurora screamed. "The rift—it's opening again!"

I turned. At the far end of the cemetery, the sky had torn wide in a new place. The wind howled, dragging ghosts and light toward it in a torrent. The Grave Moon pulsed overhead, feeding it.

Death yanked his blade free and shouted, "We can't kill him here—the Veil will collapse!"

The edges of the scythe were alive with power that burned my hands. "Then send him back!"

The Ferryman writhed, his form breaking apart, shadows flailing like wings. Andy lunged again, teeth sinking into the Ferryman's arm. Ghost pounced on the Ferryman's back.

"I'll do it," Death said.

Killion grabbed my hand again. "Channel me," he said hoarsely. "Through the bond. Take what you need."

My heart lurched. "It could burn you out completely."

He smiled, small and sharp. "Then make it count."

The Ferryman's gaze locked onto me. "Reaper," he intoned, each syllable bending the air. "When I claim you, I will no longer be death's servant. *I will be Death itself.*"

Death laughed once, low and lethal. "Position is already filled, mate."

The Ferryman staggered, then roared. His oar, blackened and slick with river light, split into two jagged blades. "You cannot stop the tide!"

I gripped Killion's hand tightly and burrowed down, down, down. The bond flared so bright it hurt to see. Our magic fused again—his dragon flame and my Grim Zero magic—spiraling up the scythe in a torrent of blinding power. Using it to infuse the blade, I grinned. "Watch me."

Ghost and Andy pinned the Ferryman down, the two of them snarling light and fury. Death's shadow wrapped around them, folding time itself, forcing the rift to respond.

The Ferryman convulsed, screaming. "I *am the river!*"

"Not anymore," I whispered.

I drove the scythe through him.

Light burst outward in a thousand shards. His form shattered into bone, shadow, and light, scattering like glass in a hurricane. The ground trembled as the rift over the cemetery tried to suck him in.

But he didn't go.

His manic laughter filled my ears. He swung his swords, bearing down on me...

Ghost lunged, grabbing hold of his cloak. Death moved with her.

Both of their gazes met mine right before they jumped into the rift with him. The edges began to pull together. My blade jerked free from my hands. It swung on its own in an arc, sending out wave after wave of magic. Both rips vanished with a sucking sound, sealed once more.

The graveyard fell silent. Real, heavy, perfect silence.

I fell to my knees, my palm burning as my blade returned to me, slapping into my grip. My hands trembled, my vision dimmed.

Killion caught me before I toppled over completely, cradling me against him. "Hey," he murmured. "You did it."

I sucked in huge gulps of air. "Barely," I whispered. I glanced around, waiting for Death and Ghost to reappear.

They didn't.

Across the lawn, Aurora stood inside her glowing circle, tears streaking down her face as Andy—still in wolf form—limped toward her. She dropped to her knees and buried her face in his fur.

There were no ghosts, only shadows. Katarina and Harlow began checking on all their nestmates.

"They'll be back any moment, right?" I asked Killion.

He knew what I meant. He peered at the spot where

the biggest rip had been. "If not," he said, "we'll go get them."

I forced a smile. "Death didn't get the last word in this time."

"That alone will make him determined to return."

"He'll find his way back." I wanted to believe it. "He always does."

Above us, the Grave Moon dimmed to silver, its shadow fading, leaving behind only the soft light of dawn creeping along the horizon.

TWENTY-TWO

Morning came too quietly.

No alarms. No howling winds or screaming ghosts. Just the hum of Danté's Grove below the penthouse windows and the faint pulse of Killion's heartbeat —an echo of mine—where my head rested against his chest.

My muscles felt like I'd been ground between millstones. Even my magic was muted. Distant.

Grim Zero was worried.

So was I.

Ghost shifted at the foot of the bed with a soft whine. When I lifted my head, her eyes were bright. Restless. She watched the shadows as if waiting for someone to step through them.

I reached down, brushing my fingers over her head. "At least you came back," I whispered. "Good girl."

Her tail gave one half-hearted thump before stilling. She pressed her muzzle to my hand. Cold and comforting, but not enough. If only she could talk and tell me what had happened after she and Death dragged the Ferryman to the other side.

My gaze slid toward the far wall. The scythe leaned there—silent, dull, the silver blade darkened to gunmetal. I hadn't wanted to leave it near the penthouse door. I'd needed it close.

Normally, its death magic whispered at the edges of my awareness. Now, there was nothing.

I sat up slowly, wincing as the movement tugged at the bandages all over my body. My head pounded, and a lump had formed. Just a mild concussion. Lucky me. I was thankful for my magic and its healing abilities. I'd be back to normal by sundown.

Killion stirred beside me, his hair mussed and his voice rough with sleep. "What time is it?"

"Late afternoon." I scanned the skyline beyond the patio doors—thin streaks of pale light tinting the glass gold. "We've slept nine hours." Nine hours of peace and every minute of it earned.

He reached for my wrist, thumb tracing the pulse there. The bond pulsed with love and worry. "You're still pale."

"So are you," I countered, forcing a smile that didn't reach my eyes. "Guess we make quite the pair."

He huffed a soft laugh. When I didn't lie back down, he propped himself on one elbow. "What is it?"

He always knew when I was hiding something—especially when it scared me. I stared at the scythe again, my magic searching for Death. The tether between us had always been a thread under my skin, his magic thunder in my bones.

It was silent.

Silence from Death was never a good thing. "I can't feel him," I said quietly.

He reached over and brushed his knuckles along my jaw. "I'm sure he's fine. Maybe he's reporting in to SMG. It will be a lengthy report."

"SMG can wait," I groused. "He shouldn't leave me hanging like this."

"I doubt he's worried about your feelings."

True. "What if..." I forced myself to contemplate it. "What if he can't get back?"

Ghost's ears flattened. She gave a low growl.

Killion sighed, sinking back against the pillows. "We'll go after him."

"You'd go back to the Ghost Lands after what happened?"

He shut his eyes. "I go where you go."

I scooted in beside him again, curling my body around his. "We give him a few more hours, and then we'll go after him, deal?"

A sigh. He rubbed my back. "First, we contact SMG and ask if he's there."

It wasn't reassurance, but it was enough to satisfy me for the moment. I kissed his cheek. "Thank you."

Pennyworth was gliding into the dining room when we emerged, balancing a silver tray piled high with enough food to feed a small army—or at least one semi-hungry reaper and her overprotective vampire mate.

"Breakfast is served," he announced, setting down plates. "Coffee, blood-orange marmalade toast, and something resembling protein for you, Mistress Chloe. For Master Killion, rare steak and a small decanter of O-negative, since you both insist on skipping proper meals after near-death experiences."

The butler could guilt-trip a corpse into eating. Ghost sprawled beneath the table, tail flicking lazily as I slid her a piece of toast. She devoured it in two bites. I played with the rest of the food, still thinking about the previous night and Death being MIA.

Killion cut into his steak, dark eyes flicking toward me. "Not hungry? Unusual."

"I'm working up to it," I said, taking a sip of coffee. I was always starving. Today, my stomach was a basket of nerves.

He gave me that look—the one that was half command, half concern. "Eat, Chloe."

I picked up my fork, glaring. "Yes, Master," I said under my breath.

The doorbell chimed. Ghost's head shot up, ears on high alert.

Pennyworth started for the door, but Aurora burst in, her arms full of jars, herbs, and what looked suspiciously like an entire tea set. "I brought reinforcements," she declared.

Andy followed, tall and weary, his T-shirt wrinkled, a gauze bandage around one hand. Despite the exhaustion, his eyes were brighter than I'd seen them in months—feral around the edges, but alive.

Behind them, Pennyworth sighed softly. "Please come in and make yourself at home."

Andy slapped him on the shoulder and trailed after Aurora, who brought her supplies to the table and set them down. Herbal infusions," she said. "For magical recalibration. We all need it."

Killion sniffed as the scent filled the air, waving off the cup she tried to hand him. "No, thanks. I'll enjoy my breakfast, if you don't mind."

"Breakfast?" She glanced at her watch. "It's nearly four p.m."

"We slept all day." I forced a smile when she handed me the cup instead. The brew smelled like old socks, and I nearly gagged. "Did you two get any rest?"

Andy winced, pressing a hand to his temple. "More like nightmares."

Aurora's expression softened. "I think the trauma of shifting after so long stirred things up."

"It's more than that." He looked up, eyes flicking between us. "I keep seeing things. Shadows moving in mirrors." His voice grew quieter with each word, as if saying it aloud made it real. "Faces—people—there one second, gone the next."

I set my mug down slowly. "Ghosts?"

Killion's voice went quiet. "Or hallucinations."

Illusions, I sent through our channel. *Like I had in the Ghost Lands.*

Andy rubbed the back of his neck. "I can't tell."

Aurora pushed a steaming mug toward him. "Drink. It'll help ground you."

He took a cautious sip and coughed. "Tastes like you stewed dirty socks."

Bingo.

"It may not taste great," she said, "but it will get rid of toxins."

I leaned my chin on my hand. "She forced me to drink a similar brew last year when my necromancy went haywire."

Andy gave me a grim smile. "I remember."

"For the record, it did help. After the sixtieth cup and minor emotional trauma."

Killion coughed into his fist. "Major trauma."

Aurora clucked her tongue. "You're all so dramatic."

Pennyworth reappeared, setting down a plate of fresh pastries with quiet authority. "Drama requires proper sustenance. Scone?"

We all took one.

For a brief, perfect moment, the chaos felt far away. The clink of silverware, the smell of cinnamon, the late afternoon light slanting through the tall windows—almost normal.

But then Andy's head jerked to look to his left. His eyes went distant. "I hear them. They're whispering," he murmured.

We all looked in the same direction. I saw nothing. Heard nothing.

"What are they saying?" I asked.

"I can't..." His voice trailed off. He blinked, seeming a million miles away. "They want my help. They're so lonely. So sad."

Aurora gripped his wrist. "Andy—look at me."

He blinked several times, eyes refocusing. "What?"

Silence fell around the table.

Finally, Killion spoke, voice soft but sure. "He's shadow-touched."

Aurora frowned. "Meaning?"

Killion's gaze shifted to me. "He has a foot in both worlds. The things he sees and hears are not hallucinations." He glanced at me. *Or illusions.*

A chill crawled down my spine. "Then what are they?"

"Spirits," Killion said simply. "Ones who can't rest. And now, they've found someone who can hear them."

"You're a tweener like me," I said. But I still didn't hear or see what he was.

His brows furrowed. "A what?"

"When you die and come back, you've walked between worlds. You're able to see and communicate with ghosts because you've walked in both dimensions."

He shook his head. "I didn't die."

"I reaped you, remember? Back before we were friends, you were a noncompliant on my list." I played with a bit of scone, remembering how he'd dodged me effectively for quite a few weeks before Christmas. "It's surprising you didn't have this problem before now. I just never thought about it."

"Your wolf died recently, too," Killion added. "And now, it has returned. Perhaps that's what has triggered your new ability."

Andy said nothing for a minute, staring at his plate.

He sat forward, meeting my eyes. "How do you deal with it? All the voices?"

"I normally only hear them when they're in reaping range." The worry in his posture made me want to reach across the table and squeeze his hand. "We need to talk to Death about this. Get his input."

"I was afraid you'd say that." He rubbed a hand over his face. "Can you call him for me?"

"I have been calling him." I sucked down more coffee, fighting off my exhaustion. "He's not answering."

Aurora tilted her head. "He hasn't come back? Checked in with you?"

I shook my head. "Not a word, and it's got me worried." I gestured at Ghost under the table. "I mean, she came back, so that's a good sign, but he's AWOL. No one's answering my messages at SMG, either. I don't know if it's intentional, or something's wrong."

Andy sipped his tea, grimacing. I could tell he was trying to ignore whatever he was hearing from the spirits. "Wrong, like what? Like, he can't get back? Or Oblivion...?"

Silence fell, heavy and filled with dread.

Pennyworth cleared his throat gently. "Would anyone care for another scone while we contemplate existential horror?"

Aurora laughed despite herself. Andy managed a grin. Even I smiled—barely.

Pennyworth whisked away the empty plates with stealth, humming a classical tune under his breath. Aurora poured another round of tea that none of us wanted, and Andy leaned back in his chair, eyes half-lidded, the wolf just behind them.

I glanced toward the window. "SMG hasn't even requested my report."

Aurora shook her head, curls bouncing. "If Mei were still in charge, she wouldn't have even let you sleep today before giving her a full account." She gave me a small smile. "You'd think they'd at least send a fruit basket for your saving existence."

Killion's jaw tightened. "At least they haven't come after the scythe again."

I took another sip of coffee. "The whole thing makes me uneasy."

That earned me a long pause. Andy's hand tightened around his mug; Aurora's gaze flicked to me, then down.

"Surely Death is fine," she said too quickly. "He always lands on his feet. Maybe he's just avoiding you."

I raised a brow. "Avoiding me? Why?"

She leaned back in her chair, the picture of breezy confidence. "Chloe, please. He's Death, and you're... Grim Zero. Being evasive and cryptic is his favorite sport because he can't handle his feelings for you."

Killion's mouth firmed. He put down his fork with a clang. "She's not wrong."

Aurora grinned, clearly encouraged. "He probably gave SMG a full report and is now skulking around some-where, annoying his other grims, and telling them all about how *he* saved us from Oblivion. You'll get a dramatic entrance any minute now—fog machine, thunder, the whole bit."

I tried to laugh, but it came out thin. Grim Zero paced inside my chest. It wasn't easy to balance her emotions with mine. She was his mate; he was her everything. I couldn't imagine how scared she was right now. Well, actually, I could. Her emotional trauma was making my head spin. "That would be just like him," I forced out, trying to sound like me.

Andy set down his mug. "He's been gone before, right? Between missions?"

"Yeah, but I've always been able to sense him. I mean, because I work for him as a grim, there was always this connection, and because of Grim Zero. She has a direct bond with him. Now it's just..." I touched my sternum. "Gone."

Aurora reached across the table and squeezed my hand. "He's fine," she said again, gentler this time. "You can't get rid of him that easily."

Killion drank his coffee, mouth still grim. "He's an ancient cosmic being with the emotional maturity of a brick wall, but I, too, believe something is off."

Aurora's smile faltered. "You think the Ferryman or Oblivion has him? That they're both still alive?"

Killion hesitated, then exhaled slowly. "We don't know if he was able to destroy either entity. We only returned them to where they belonged. If the Veil is truly sealed, and he's still not back, it might mean he's trapped there."

"Trapped?" Aurora repeated, eyes widening. "You're saying Death is stuck in his own domain?"

Killion nodded. "It's possible. The Ferryman had

rewritten parts of the Veil with his corruption. Death might be stuck due to that."

The air went cold, the words hanging heavy between us. My chest contracted hard.

Aurora broke the silence first, trying for a teasing tone that didn't quite stick. "If anyone can out-stubborn the afterlife, it's him."

I smiled weakly. "He needs to hurry up and prove it."

Ghost made a soft, uneasy whine under the table. The sound curled through me, low and sad, and I found myself gripping my mug too tightly. "He and I destroyed several anchors—sanctums—when we were in the corrupted version of the Ghost Lands. They're dimensional stabilizers built to regulate the flow of souls between realms, only they weren't active any longer, according to him. The Ferryman was using them, though, so we needed to destroy them. Is it possible that it backfired somehow, and that's contributing to him not being able to travel between the dimensions?"

Killion's hand brushed mine. "We'll find him," he said. "One way or another."

Aurora stood, gathering her things. "I'll dig through my archives—see if there's anything about these sanctums and how their destruction might affect dimensional travel."

"Thanks," I said softly.

Andy offered a lopsided grin. "Besides, the world's quieter without him. Maybe enjoy that while it lasts."

Aurora elbowed him. "Ignore him. He's never liked Death."

They gathered their things, Aurora tucking a pouch of herbs into my hand. "For focus," she said, winking. "And no, it doesn't smell like dirty socks."

"I'll be the judge of that," I said, forcing a smile.

Pennyworth escorted them out. When the door closed, the silence settled deep and uneasy. "Shall I light a fire and pour a nice cabernet, Master?"

Killion quirked a brow at me. I shook my head. "I'm going to reach out to SMG again."

And if I didn't get a response, I was going to start burning things down.

TWENTY-THREE

The silence after Aurora and Andy left felt heavy. The smell of cinnamon lingered in the air, mingling with Killion's half-finished steak.

Ghost pawed at my leg, and I lifted her into my lap. Pennyworth brought me my phone to message SMG, but I didn't need it.

Killion reached for his glass but froze halfway as light shimmered above the table—blue, fractured, like moonlight through water. Mei Han's image flickered to life in complete holographic form, projected right between us.

She wavered, half-transparent. "Don't speak—just listen."

Killion's hand dropped from his glass. "What the—"

Mei's eyes flicked toward him. "This channel isn't secure." Her voice cracked through static, brittle as glass. "I shouldn't even be contacting you."

My stomach dropped. "What's going on?"

Mei's face tightened. "Death is being held at SMG headquarters."

I dropped my phone, startling Ghost. "What?"

"Held how?" Killion asked. "As in, he's imprisoned?"

"They're calling it a quarantine, but they've jailed him." Her eyes darted to something off-screen, back to me. "He's expected to go before the board in an hour to explain what happened with the Ferryman."

I shot to my feet, Ghost landing on the floor. "We just saved everyone from being annihilated. Why in the reapers would they jail him?"

Mei gave a solemn nod. "The new director—Ethan Ashlar—has put together a task force to audit and investigate all operations since you became Grim 281."

My pulse ticked up. "Were they going to let me know they were investigating me again? I thought we put all of this to rest after Sylvie audited me."

"Ashlar doesn't want you alerted. He feels you can... manipulate...Death. That you compelled Sylvie to turn in those reports to clear your name. He wants this investigation done without you knowing."

My knees went loose. I had to sit again. "I don't suppose you influenced that?"

Her face pinched. "You've broken dozens of rules and regulations. We all know that. Since the night you donned the robes, Killion and Death have as well. I simply came to warn you—Ashlar is after you. He's ten times worse than me, and he thinks you're unstable, a threat, and he'll be coming for the scythe, too."

Killion's entire posture changed—predatory, protective. I dropped my head into my hands. "Not this again."

Mei's image flickered again, making her look thinner, tired. "The board will move fast once the ruling comes down. Be prepared."

"This is insane."

She glanced over her shoulder. Her face drained of what little color the hologram displayed. "I have to go. He's coming."

"Mei, wait—"

The blue light winked out.

"Ashlar will regret it if he so much as touches Death," I growled.

Killion pushed his glass away. "He'll regret it even more if he touches you."

"We need to be proactive. Go to SMG." I stood again. Ghost danced at my feet. "What do you say to crashing that board meeting, Master?"

Killion stared at me for a long moment, totally calm and still. I could see him calculating the odds of us walking out of SMG if we went after Death or tried to reason with the board. "I don't suppose I can talk you out of it?"

That meant, in his estimation, the odds were poor. Fair enough. "I'm not saying we go in without a plan."

The side of his mouth quirked. "I have an idea."

Of course he did. He was the master strategist. "I'm all ears."

He leaned back. "We know someone inside SMG who owes you a favor."

I frowned. "We do?"

"A clerk."

I searched my mind, came up blank. "Who are you talking about?"

His mouth tilted slightly. "A nervous, highly under-paid clerk who has a bad habit of knowing things he shouldn't."

"Tinder," I said, grabbing my phone.

Killion stopped me. "We need to use a method that SMG can't track."

He placed a call to Harlow, and within five minutes, a tall, lanky man wearing a cockeyed newspaper boy hat landed in our living room. His skin was pale, his beard patchy, and he looked like he hadn't slept in a year.

"Tinder," I said, "you look terrible."

"Lovely to see you, too, Grim 281." His British lilt was present, but softer than usual. He rubbed the back of his neck. "You're radioactive, you know. My inbox has been a funeral since the Ferryman business."

"Radioactive?" Killion asked dryly. "That would be an improvement."

Tinder flinched. "Killion. Always a pleasure. Do tell me you're not planning to kill anyone in the next five minutes?"

Killion didn't so much as blink. "No promises."

I clutched my scythe, refusing to be parted with it. "Mei told us Death's being held in a jail cell at SMG. What do you know?"

Tinder's eyes darted side to side, as if expecting his own shadow to report him. "More than I should. The board meeting is a front—just for show. They've already decided to keep him contained indefinitely."

Killion's jaw tightened. "Indefinitely." It was said as if he questioned everything about that adverb.

"Until they can 'verify the stability of the Veil,'" Tinder quoted, fingers making air quotes. "Which, between us, is bureaucratic nonsense for forever."

The word landed like a blade point-down in my chest. "He's Death. They can't do that."

He shrugged. "They'll find a replacement."

I gripped the scythe tighter. "Where is he being held?"

Tinder picked at his chin. "In the containment vault beneath HQ. It's a pocket dimension. Top-level clearance only. They call it the Vault of Silence."

My pulse stumbled, but this explained why I couldn't feel him. Why he couldn't answer my messages. "How do you know this?"

He smiled faintly. "Because I'm the one who files the requisition orders for its maintenance. I see the names that are on those lists." The pride in his voice was small but stubborn.

"Tell me you know how to open it," I said.

Tinder hesitated, his gaze flicking to the scythe. "You already have the key."

The scythe warmed in my palm. "This?"

He nodded. "The inner seal was designed long ago and tied to Death's energy signature. It can only be opened by something forged in that same resonance.

Ashlar has the official master key, but..." He eyed my weapon. "You have one, too."

My pulse picked up. "The First Blade."

"Precisely," Tinder said.

Killion's gaze slid to me. "That's the real reason why Ashlar wants it."

Tinder grimaced. "Ashlar's a figurehead, but he's smart. Devious. He doesn't want anyone to have more control than he does."

I paced in front of the fireplace hearth and Ghost's bed. "So I can break Death out of jail."

Tinder shifted. "What they're doing to him isn't right, and I want to help, but if you're considering it, you should know the moment you breach that vault, they'll know. Every alarm in the building will go off. And the Board will classify you both as hostile entities."

"I think we're past that," I said. "I can live with it."

"No, you can't," Tinder said sharply. The usual fidgeting stilled, his voice suddenly grave. "You have no idea what they'll do to keep Death contained. If you try to break him out, they'll label you as 'compromised' and throw you in with him. You'll lose everything, Grave Girl."

Killion folded his arms. "He's right."

I turned on him. "You can't seriously be siding with him."

"I'm siding with reason. We can't fight an institution that owns every gate between life and death. If we break Death out of jail, we're fugitives forever, and you can't hide from SMG."

Tinder nodded. "Trust me, there's nowhere you can hide where their sensors won't find you. And the scythe's energy signature is unique since it's tied to the Veil."

I slammed my palm on the mantle. "I have to free Death so we can both talk to them, explain everything."

Killion rested a hand at the base of my neck. His magic engulfed me, warm and gentle. "Offer cooperation," he said. "If Ashlar wants power, then you go in as an ally, not a threat. Make him think you'll share your power with him, which is extraordinary and will be hard for him to pass up. Convince him he needs it and you to restore Universal Balance. Tell him your experience with the Ferryman and the Veil showed you that it's time to change your ways."

Tinder made a face. "That might work, assuming he lets you in the front door."

Killion ignored him, rubbing circles on my back. "We can't outrun them, and we can't outfight them, Chloe. But we can outmaneuver them. Agree to his terms. Convince him that keeping you and Death active in the world will be an asset to his plans."

I stared at him, thinking it over. "If he'll even consider it, he'll insist that I follow every protocol to the letter. I'd rather quit."

"Call it strategy," he said quietly. "If you resign, he'll still keep Death locked away, but if you offer to help him and go by the rules, you'll have leverage."

"Leverage?" I repeated, incredulous. "He's got the power to call in my life contract, Killion."

He knew what that meant—that he was on the chopping block, too. "All the more reason for the two of us to become the tip of Ashlar's spear. What he wants done, we'll do."

Tinder scrubbed his face with both hands. "I can't believe I'm saying this, but the vampire's right. Ashlar's by-the-book, but he's not a monster. If you go in calm and prove you can be useful, he might listen."

I slumped against Killion. "I hate this plan."

"I know," he said. "But you know it's the best one."

Ghost whined softly, picking up on my worry. Tinder checked his elaborate clockwork watch. "You don't have much time. The board meeting starts in two."

"I thought we had at least thirty minutes," I said.

He shook his head. "The official start time is half an hour from now, but they'll be done long before that. It's happening, like now. If you're doing this, walk in as if you belong there. I'll transport you if you swear not to get me fired."

Heart now racing, I held up the scythe. There wasn't any more time to plan. "On my blade, I swear it."

Killion grabbed his jacket. I tucked Ghost under my arm. "Ready."

Tinder reached for us, and the world spun.

TWENTY-FOUR

The chamber doors loomed like the gates of an ancient tomb. Black stone veined with silver sigils, taller than any cathedral door I'd ever seen. The sigils pulsed with contained power—wards meant to keep mortals out, and something far older in.

Killion stood beside me, calm and deadly quiet. Ghost crouched low between us, her fur gleaming faint blue under the sterile overhead lights. The hum of the elevator faded behind us, leaving only the heartbeat of the building—a low, rhythmic thrum like the pulse of the Veil.

"Ready?" Killion asked quietly.

I had been. Now, standing here, I was having second thoughts. This was it—I had to convince the people on the other side of these doors that I was willing to be the obedient grim they wanted. I had to do whatever was necessary to free Death and make sure no one ended my soul contract—and therefore Killion's Undead life—early. "Absolutely," I murmured, and shoved at the doors.

They were heavy and resisted. I shoved harder, a sudden rush of strength making them shudder and fly open.

The chamber was a cathedral of glass, iron, and bone —older than any mortal government—vast, and lit by soft white fire in sconces carved from bone. The air that flowed out was colder than the grave.

Tiered seats curved upward in a half-circle, filled with dozens—no, hundreds—of figures in pale robes. Shadows whispered between them like the murmurs of the dead.

At the center of the chamber stood a single circle of light—and within it, one chair.

My heart hitched. Grim Zero froze inside my chest.

Death sat, bound by concentric bands of light wards. The restraints were made of words and willpower, a hundred old oaths twisted into chains. His long coat hung in tatters; his usually sharp posture was slumped. He looked...smaller than I'd ever seen him. The shadows that were usually his allies curled close, trapped against his skin.

A tall man stood on the dais above him, speaking to the assembly. Mid-forties, silvering at the temples, eyes as gray and cool as a storm cloud. His suit was impeccable, no tie, not a single wrinkle. Even his stillness felt like control.

Ethan Ashlar. SMG's new director.

He was in the middle of some polished speech about

'containment,' 'universal equilibrium,' and 'the necessity of consequence' when the crash of the doors cut him off.

The echo rolled through the chamber. Conversations stopped. A thousand eyes turned our way.

Killion and I walked in step, Ghost gliding between us. I let my scythe blade screech against the marble floor with every stride—a deliberate, unhurried rhythm.

Death sat up and swiveled, glowering with narrowed eyes when they landed on me.

We stopped just shy of the central ring. Ashlar simply tilted his head, assessing me the way a hawk measures distance before the dive. "Grim 281." His voice was smooth as glass. "You're interrupting a closed tribunal."

"Then open it," I said. My voice carried, clear and sharp.

Death shook his head. "For reapers' sake. What are you—"

I shot him a look and hissed, "Rescuing you. Again."

Ashlar leaned on his podium, his curious stare cunning. "I don't know how you found out about this meeting or managed to barge in, but you are aware this is classified above your clearance level."

I lifted my chin. "I'm aware you're holding my superior in violation of the same protocols you claim to defend." Killion cleared his throat, reminding me to play nice. I forced myself to soften my voice. "And I'm here to throw myself on the mercy of the board."

A ripple of whispers traveled through the seats. The scythe throbbed against my palm. Death frowned.

Ashlar stepped down from his perch and strolled to a spot a few paces away. "Is that so?"

"Let's not play games." I tapped the scythe against my leg, and as expected, his gaze zeroed in on it. "You intentionally planned to keep me out of this because you know Death is not to blame for the universal imbalance we're experiencing. You really want to put *me* in that jail cell. But let me guess, when he showed up to report on our war with the Ferryman and Oblivion—which we won, by the way. You can thank me later—you decided to make him the scapegoat for my wrongdoings. Not very smart, if you ask me, and that violates his rights."

Death's mouth twitched—half warning, half approval.

Ashlar's eyes narrowed, no longer tempered with curiosity. "You are walking a dangerous line, Grim 281."

Killion's quiet baritone cut through the charged silence. "You might want to let her speak, Director. She's here with a proposal you'll find advantageous."

Ashlar studied him for one long beat, then shifted his gaze back to me. Still calculating. Curious once more. "Very well, Reaper. You have the floor."

I tightened my grip on the scythe, the weight of every watching soul pressing down before I stepped into the light ring.

Apparently, that shocked the crowd, a collective gasp echoing in the chamber. I glanced at Killion. In my head, he said, *Your power defies theirs. Use it to your advantage. Show them they need you.*

I turned back to my audience. "If blame's the

currency here, spend it on me," I said, voice steady. "Death didn't break your rules—I did. He's the reason the rest of us are still breathing."

Death's voice hammered the air behind me. "Chloe, this isn't necessary."

I didn't acknowledge him. "He told me to follow protocol every single time. I didn't. I bent the rules, crossed lines, and still, he had my back. In the field that can mean the difference between life and, well, death."

A few chuckles gave me confidence. Death groaned under his breath. I cradled the scythe. My words echoed through the chamber, climbing the iron ribs of the ceiling and vanishing into the endless dark. "If that's a crime, make me the example."

Every robe-clad figure watched me, unblinking, as if weighing the worth of my soul against the weight of my sins.

I took a breath, slow and deliberate. "I'm here to tell you I've seen what my rebellion has done. I've seen the cracks in the Veil, the cost of chaos. I understand now— power without balance destroys everything it touches."

Ashlar kept glancing at the scythe and had to draw his attention back to me. "Go on."

The scythe hummed to life as I raised it. Pale silver light spilled across the marble, touching the sigils holding Death. He lifted his chin, just enough that our eyes met, shadow and starlight flickering between us.

"You want order restored?" I planted my feet and channeled Killion. "I'll restore it. I'll follow the book, the law, the hierarchy—whatever you need." I tipped the blade toward Ashlar, its glow glinting off his calm, unreadable eyes. "And I'm not Grim 281. I'm Grim Zero —the most powerful ally, outside of Death himself, that you'll ever have."

For a heartbeat, no one breathed. Even the firelight in the sconces seemed to hesitate, caught between burning and bowing.

Ashlar studied me in silence, fingers steepled, his expression impossible to read. Around him, the Board shifted like one massive hive mind considering a new idea.

"You make a compelling case, Grim Zero," he said, each word precise, putting particular emphasis on my name. "And yet, one cannot help but question your motives."

I met his gaze head-on. Inside my chest, Grim Zero stirred, egging me on. She knew we had him. We just needed to close the deal. "My motive is simple—I owe Death everything. I'm here to ask you to set him free."

"Is it? Simple?" Ashlar's tone was mild, but it pressed like a blade against my skin, threatening. "You've flouted nearly every directive SMG has placed upon you since your assignment began. You wield your scythe as if it were your own to command, rather than the property of this organization. You fraternize with assets,"—his gaze flicked to Killion—"who interfere with Universal Balance protocols, and repeatedly compromise the chain of command." His pause stretched. "And now, you stand here invoking mercy."

Mercy, no. I lifted my chin. "I'm here to make amends and take responsibility."

The whispering rose again through the chamber.

Ashlar folded his hands behind his back and began pacing a slow circle around Death and me. "Tell me, then, *Grim Zero*...what changed? Why this sudden desire for obedience?"

I took a long breath. I needed to appear contrite and humbled, even though I wanted to cut through Death's restraints and tell them all off. "I finally understand what's at stake. I've seen the Veil torn open. I've seen Oblivion trying to claw its way through. I thought doing things my way made me stronger—but it nearly unmade everything."

I turned toward the gathered Board, their pale faces flickering in the sconce light. "You don't need a rule-breaker. You need a reaper who understands the cost of imbalance. I am that now."

Ashlar stopped beside Death's circle, eyeing him and my presence inside it. "You ask this council to pardon your superior, who failed to keep you in line, when it was both of your actions that triggered the collapse in the first place?"

Not exactly how I saw it, but I subverted my gaze, hoping I appeared repentant. "Death didn't abandon me when he should have. He taught me what it means to carry the weight of the scythe—and how to wield it without losing myself. Everything I know about balance, I learned from him."

Death finally spoke, voice rough but proud. "Everything she did, she did with the best intentions."

Ashlar's head tilted slightly, eyes narrowing. "You, of all entities, defending a mortal who has nearly broken the order of the cosmos?"

Death smiled faintly. I was barely human anymore, and we both knew it. "It's not the first time a mortal has changed the cosmos. It won't be the last."

That earned a ripple of murmurs—some approval, more outrage.

Ashlar raised a hand. The room stilled. His gaze flicked back to me and briefly took in the scythe. He hid his eagerness for it well, but I saw it flash in his eyes every time they landed on the blade. "You claim reform. You claim understanding." He turned to address the Board. "Shall we see if her words hold weight?"

A pulse of power rippled through the chamber. The robed figures rose in unison, hands glowing faintly as they cast their votes. It was all silent, and I shifted from one foot to another, wondering what verdict they were coming to.

Finally, Ashlar turned back to me, unreadable. "The council has voted to put you on probation." He stepped closer, voice lowering. "You and Death will remain under observation for the next lunar cycle. During that time, your actions will determine your continued employment —and your continued existence."

Death exhaled, a soft sound that might've been relief.

Ashlar continued, his tone flattening into a formal decree. "Probation begins immediately. Any further deviation from established protocols will result in both of you being permanently unbound from this realm." His gaze cut briefly to Killion. "And your bonded companion will follow."

My breath caught, but I didn't flinch. "Understood."

Ashlar nodded once. "Good. Then we are finished here."

He turned as if to dismiss us—then hesitated. "Grim Zero," he said without looking back. "A word. In private."

He disappeared behind a door to the left. It gave a soft, metallic hiss.

Death's eyes met mine. For the first time since I'd met him, I saw something close to fear.

"What does he want?" I whispered.

"I don't know," he said, as the light bonds vanished and Killion edged closer to me. Death stood, rubbing his wrists. "Just don't screw up."

I punched him on his massive bicep. "Great pep-talk, boss. Oh, and I just threw myself on my sword for you. You're free now because of me. You can thank me later," I repeated.

He rolled his eyes.

Killion squeezed my hand. "Be careful."

I glanced at the door where Ashlar had disappeared. I had the feeling I knew exactly what he wanted. I twirled the blade. "Don't worry. I've got this. Come on, Ghost. Let's go."

I went through the door and was instantly outside Mei's former office. The door stood open. I stepped inside.

The glass walls offered an endless panorama of jagged white ridges and shadowed valleys. Frost filmed the corners of the floor-to-ceiling panes. Snow crunched faintly beneath my boots, and Ghost pushed her nose through it.

Ashlar sat at the desk—sleek black metal now, no trace of Mei's plants or personal touches. He saw me assessing this. "Leadership is temporary when you go outside the law."

I didn't know what to make of that, so I said nothing.

He gestured toward the chair opposite his. "Sit."

Ghost settled at my feet as I obeyed, still acting my part. I laid the scythe in my lap.

"You surprised me, Chloe," he said finally. "If you don't mind me calling you that."

I did, but I gave him a gracious smile. It was less formal —was he trying to be seen as my confidant now? "Not at all."

"You could have hidden. Instead, you came back."

"Running isn't my thing."

He gave a faint smile, eyes cool but searching my face. "You meant what you said in that chamber—about restoring order?"

"Yes." I straightened. "I want to effect change. I just don't want to be a political pawn like Mei tried to make me."

"I don't need pawns." He turned toward the glass, watching the clouds drift by. "I need someone who can see what I can't."

What exactly did that mean? "I'm a tribred, sir, but I'm not psychic."

He huffed a soft breath—almost a laugh. "A very unique entity. That makes you a liability...and an opportunity."

He was as smart as Tinder had claimed. Smart, cunning, and definitely up to something. Ghost whined, sensing it, too. Time to find out what. "You want to...capitalize on that."

"Yes." He faced me fully again, but didn't look at the scythe this time. I wondered what that was costing him in willpower. "I'm offering you a chance to do more than repair the damage you've done."

I folded my arms. "Can you be more specific? As I said, I'm not psychic."

He touched the glass wall, and a map unfolded across it—streams of light forming intricate constellations. "This is my new Universal Balance Initiative. Every crossing soul, every spectral tether, every ripple in the Veil runs through this network. Since the Ferryman's corruption and your destruction of the Sanctums, it's become highly unstable."

The lights flickered, twisting in strange, broken patterns.

"Death's imprisonment was a precaution," he continued. "We had to ensure he wasn't tainted by what the Ferryman left behind."

"He's not," I said.

"No," Ashlar agreed, "but the corruption remains.

The Ferryman's destruction disrupted something older—something feeding on the fractures in the Veil."

"Oblivion," I breathed.

"Possibly." He met my eyes. "Whatever it is, it's growing. For now, that's not your concern. There's something...more sensitive...I'd like you to handle for me."

The clouds outside churned, a storm swirling around the peaks.

I kept my voice steady. "What?"

He clasped his hands behind his back, his tone smooth and deliberate. "You'll perform one reap for the board. A sanctioned execution."

My stomach dropped. "What?" He raised one brow, a challenge. I swallowed. "Of who?"

Ashlar's gray eyes met mine, calm and calculating. "Mei Han."

I almost fell out of the chair. "You can't be serious."

"I'm always serious." He moved closer, close enough that I could see the faint network of silver veins at his temples. "Director Han has multiple serious counts against her."

"She's under review," I said. "Not sentenced."

"Yet," he replied softly. "The board will debate her fate in three days. But if you carry out the reap before then, she forfeits any appeal or possibility of pardon. You know what she's done. She doesn't deserve either."

The realization hit me all at once. "You want her gone before she can defend herself."

He didn't deny it. "She's immortal, technically. The

Veil has no claim over her unless you—Grim Zero—deliver it. No one else can."

Shock strangled my breath. I couldn't believe my ears. "You're asking me to—what? Murder her before the hearing?"

"Terminate an anomaly," he corrected. "She's outlived her usefulness and represents a threat to the chain of command."

A threat to him.

Kill, the scythe said.

I had no words. Mei wasn't a friend, and yes, she'd committed some nasty crimes, but this was too much. "She deserves her day in court."

Ashlar's gaze was steady, pitiless. "Then Death will remain in custody. The board will interpret your hesitation as further evidence of insubordination. Your contract —and your vampire—will be nullified."

Nullified—how...tidy.

Killion's voice flared through our bond, low and furious: *He's using you.*

Ghost pressed against my leg, ears flattened. *I know*, I replied, *but what can I do?*

I forced a breath, nails biting into my palms. "You're afraid of her," I said quietly. "You think Mei will expose whatever it is *you're* hiding and usurp you. She'll get her job back."

Ashlar smiled, but it didn't reach his eyes. "You have an overactive imagination, my young reaper. I'm an open book. But balance requires pruning. We can't have weeds in the garden, Chloe."

Back to being my friend. *Not.* "I'm not your gardener."

"But you are," he said with that same cunning smile. "You are the scythe." His gaze finally dropped to the blade again, and I saw the desire in his eyes. He wanted to wield it, but knew it wouldn't let him.

He turned back toward the window, hands clasped behind his back, his reflection merging with the storm. "So," he said, voice taunting and eager at the same time. "Will you accept this assignment...or do I terminate your soul contract?"

The glass walls shuddered under a distant thunderclap. I stared at Ashlar's reflection in the window—the storm bleeding light across the mountains—and felt the scythe hum in my lap, its silver edge pulsing. It was gentle, supportive, as if it knew the turmoil in my heart.

I would do anything to protect Killion. Ashlar knew it, too. He *was* using me and preying on my biggest weakness to force me into this.

I hated being manipulated, controlled. I wouldn't tarnish my soul by killing an innocent whose soul contract hadn't expired. I didn't know for sure that Mei even had a soul, but either way, this wasn't justice, and I hated being a part of it.

But Ashlar wasn't the only smart, cunning person in the room. I stood, gripping the scythe, and smiled. "I accept the assignment, sir."

His reflection smiled back. "You have seventy-two hours, Grim Zero. Don't let me down."

TWENTY-FIVE

Death brought the three of us, plus Ghost, to the Catholic Church. The nave was dark, and Killion flicked his wrist, lighting the lamps.

St. Anne stared down at us as Death went to one of the pews and lay down with a heavy, resigned sigh. I could feel his exhaustion in my own bones.

Shadows flickered over the statue's face. The space was cold and quiet, except for the clacking of Ghost's nails on the floor.

Katarina burst in, and Killion went to intercept her, leading her back out and closing the door behind them. I figured he was filling her in.

Death shut his eyes and pinched the bridge of his nose. His voice was hushed, ragged. "You shouldn't have come."

My thoughts were swirling. I paced, not knowing what to do. "Did you think I would just leave you there?"

"I thought you were smarter than to fall for his manipulations."

The table and chairs were too far away to make use of, so I hovered near him, pacing the length of the bench. "You guessed wrong. What manipulations are you talking about?"

Killion returned, his magic wrapping around me like a hug. His eyes were fierce, boring into me. Through our bond, he had eavesdropped on my conversation with the new director, and his anger felt like spikes directed at the man.

Death kept his eyes closed, his arm falling to his side. Another weighted sigh parted his lips, this one filled with disappointment. "I was the bait to get you there. He knew if he held me prisoner, you'd come."

I stopped, frowning down at him. Ghost sniffed around one of the torture contraptions. My scythe was quiet, but my grip was still tight, desperate. "He wanted me to come to SMG? Why didn't he just ask me to?"

"Because everything is a game to him. He thinks he's smarter than the rest of us, and he likes to feel like a puppeteer, pulling the strings."

I glanced at Killion. "We didn't even know where you were until Tinder told us."

Ghost jumped up on Death's stomach. He stroked her head. Even that small action seemed to take enormous strength from him. She licked his cheek, sensing that something was wrong. "It was all part of his plan," Death murmured. "He wanted to use me to trick you into doing his bidding."

"It seems he succeeded," Killion said.

Death opened his eyes, meeting mine. "What have you done?"

"You're saying all of this was some grand scheme of his?" I shook my head, then let it fall back and stared up at the ceiling. "There's no way he could've known that Mei would—"

Death sat up and deposited Ghost onto the floor. "Don't underestimate him." Placing his elbows on his knees, he sank his head into his hands. "Now, tell me what you agreed to do for him."

My stomach churned. I stepped back, turned, and paced to St. Anne.

He raised his head. "Chloe."

I glanced back but couldn't hold his gaze, dropping mine to the floor. "He wants me to be his personal assassin."

Death leaned back, making the pew creak. His voice dropped another octave. "Who does he want you to kill?"

My throat went dry. I forced oxygen into my lungs and exhaled sharply. "Mei."

Silence fell. I peeked at him.

His face registered shock. He rubbed a hand over it and shook his head. "That dirty piece of cosmic trash. He tried to get me to do it." He met my gaze again. "I said no. That's why he threw me in that containment cell and used me as bait to get to you."

There was accusation and challenge in his eyes. It was nearly as bad as Ashlar's coercion. I held my ground.

"I didn't have a choice. He threatened to end my soul contract if I disagreed."

Killion came to stand next to me. "We'll figure something out."

"Mei has been behind a lot of sketchy stuff," Death said, "but what he's doing isn't justice. It's vengeance."

I toyed with the blade. "I think it's a preemptive strike."

Both males focused on me. "How so?" Death asked.

"I don't think Mei is as guilty as we might believe. Yes, we have evidence that points to her being involved in soul manipulation, but what if he's been behind some of it? He wants to take her out before she has a chance to prove her innocence or regain any kind of position again with SMG."

Death took this in. "It sounds like something he would do, but what makes you think Mei is innocent of anything?"

Ghost sat next to him, wagging her tail at me. I held up the scythe. "She stole this from SMG and brought it to me during our fight. She knew I would need it to seal the rip."

A shake of his head. "Ashlar *allowed* her to steal it. Trust me, after I nicked it once, it was under an impossible lock system. There's no way she could have gotten to it, much less gotten out of SMG, without help."

Killion crossed his arms, face hardening. "You're saying the new director has manipulated this whole thing since the beginning."

Death nodded once, resting his arms on the back of

the pew and kicking one ankle up over the opposite knee. "He threatened to feed me to Oblivion when I wouldn't agree to his demands. Then he realized exactly what that would unleash."

The implications were staggering. "If he erased death," I murmured, "everyone and everything that's ever died on this planet would come to life again."

Another nod. He still wore his tattered coat, and his eyes seemed hollow, the light from the lamps unable to reach his face. Grim Zero wanted to go to him. To caress his cheek. Take his hand in hers. "I chained the Ferryman in his own river—but Oblivion can't be destroyed," he said. "Ashlar wants to harness that power. He simply hasn't figured out how to do it yet."

Yet. Meaning, he would.

Now, I needed to sit. "So by getting Mei removed from her position as director, we've managed to pave the way for a worse evil to take her place."

"What is his ultimate plan?" Killion asked.

Death spread his hands, palms up. "What do all power-hungry megalomaniacs seek?"

I clenched the blade. "Power. Don't these idiots ever get enough?"

Killion held up a finger. "He wants the *ultimate* power."

Death nodded. "He wants absolute control over life and death. Over all souls, ours included."

They both looked at me. I suddenly felt like I was drowning. "And if he controls me, he'll gain that power."

"You're now his weapon, wielding the assassin's blade," Killion said quietly.

"Grave bound," Death said.

I stood, too antsy to stay seated. "What does that mean?"

"If you use the scythe for an unsanctioned reaping—a hit basically—your soul is forever bound to the ultimate grave. That containment center at SMG? That looks like a garden compared to what you'll be thrown in."

"A version of what Christians call purgatory?" Killion asked.

"Or hell. Take your pick." Death sat forward and dropped his head into his hands. "But if you don't do what he wants, he'll end your contract."

I didn't know what to say. Ghost bounded off the pew and followed me as I took up my route to St. Anne and back again. "Others have tried to steal my blade and make me do their bidding. I've outsmarted all of them."

Death shook his head. "None of them were in charge of souls. *Your* soul."

Killion watched me pace, but through the connection, I knew he was calculating our next move. "How do we stop him?"

Words I never thought I'd hear Death say spilled from his mouth without hesitation. "I don't know."

"Oh, come on," I said, gripping the blade handle desperately again, needing something to hang onto. "There has to be a way."

"We need time, allies, and leverage. Dangling your soul contract in front of you is to keep you in line," Killion said to me. "But he won't kill you. He needs you. Your bond with the First Blade is unique. Other reapers have been able to use it, but not like you."

"So I do have leverage."

Death dropped his focus to my blade. "Don't get cocky. Ashlar may have allies and strategies we haven't considered yet. We need to bide our time and see what happens. Study him. Figure out how deep his influence goes with the board."

"I don't have time," I told them. "He gave me seventy-two hours to reap Mei."

Both males blanched.

Katarina entered with a tray of steaming coffee and sandwiches cut into triangles. She set it on the former sacrament table, nodded at Killion, and disappeared again.

The smell of coffee usually invigorated me. My stomach was twisting too much to consider it.

Death grabbed half a sandwich and downed a cup of coffee. "He's testing your loyalty. Putting pressure on you from the beginning, so you don't have time to find a way out."

Killion leaned against the dais, his calm voice cutting through my rising alarm. "Then we need to decide whether to defy him outright or play along long enough to learn what he's hiding."

Death glared at him. "Chloe's not becoming his pawn."

"She already is. We all are. SMG owns all of us, and Ashlar can end us whenever he wishes."

"What kind of proof will he need?" I asked Death. "Of Mei's death? Her body?"

"She's immortal, you know."

"Answer the question. Do I have to produce her dead form?"

He finished off another sandwich. "Her head will probably do."

My stomach flipped. "Decapitate her?" I squeaked.

He brushed crumbs from his hands. "That's how you end an immortal, Chloe. That's how they ended Grim Zero in her original form."

Inside my chest, she squirmed.

Killion drummed his fingers on the dais. "We can't win this playing by his rules. The only way to beat a man like Ashlar is to make him underestimate you."

"My thoughts, too," I said, "but how? I can't fake Mei's death. Not if he needs her head as proof."

Death gave a wicked smile. "Don't pretend. Do it."

"Are you insane?" I asked. "Not only is that a horrible thing to do, I don't want to end up grave bound."

"We're talking Universal Balance. To buy time and take Ashlar down, play your part. Mei is expendable compared to the subjugation of billions of other souls. Killion and I will figure out how to break the grave binding."

Killion looked unconvinced. "That's a dangerous game. You'll be walking a blade edge."

I lifted the scythe, light flickering off it. "Story of my life."

Outside, a cold wind rattled the stained glass windows. The still full moon cut through the cracks.

Death met my gaze. "If you decide to play his game, you'll need allies who aren't bound by the Veil."

I picked up Ghost and hugged her. "Like who?"

"Me, others I know."

"You're volunteering?"

His smile was small, dangerous. "I'm leading the charge."

"Is Mei bound by it?"

A shake of his head.

Killion's hand brushed mine. "Whatever you decide, I'm with you."

I looked between them—Death, Killion, the scythe, Ghost. The memory of Mei helping me surfaced, of her directing us to the SMG to rescue Death. Was she nothing but a pawn in Ashlar's plan, or was she a co-conspirator? One Ashlar now wanted to disappear? "Then I guess I need to decide whether I'm an assassin... or a revolutionary."

The scythe shivered in my hand, eager to see which one I'd choose.

DON'T MISS *the next Accidental Reaper story, Grave Bound, coming summer of 2026!*

FREE URBAN FANTASY! GET REVENGE IS SWEET, KALI SWEET URBAN FANTASY FREE

Step into the thrilling world of the *Kali Sweet* series —a snarky, fast-paced urban fantasy adventure packed with vampires, shifters, demons, angels, and a fierce heroine you won't forget!

If you're a fan of paranormal books featuring strong female leads with razor-sharp wit, sizzling romance, and jaw-dropping twists, this series is for you.

Dive into a world where the supernatural collides with high-stakes drama. Kali Sweet isn't your typical heroine—she's a no-nonsense, supernatural-busting force to be reckoned with. Whether she's outsmarting vampires, taking down rogue shifters, or facing off against celestial beings, Kali's brand of snark and courage will have you hooked from page one.

Fans of urban fantasy series like *The Dresden Files*, *Mercy Thompson*, or *Kate Daniels* will love the Kali Sweet series. Watch now to experience the magic, humor, and danger that define this unforgettable paranormal universe.

📚 Don't miss the chance to start your next favorite urban fantasy series. Click here to grab your FREE copy of Revenge Is Sweet today!

Listen to the series on the Eleven Reader Publishing App!

Listen to the series on the Eleven Reader Publishing App!

**Listen to the series on the Eleven Reader
Publishing App!**

COZY MYSTERIES (WRITING AS NYX HALLIWELL)

Sister Witches Of Raven Falls Mystery Series

Of Potions and Portents

Of Curses and Charms

Of Stars and Spells

Of Spirits and Superstition

Confessions of a Closet Medium Series

Pumpkins & Poltergeists

Magic & Mistletoe

Hearts & Haunts

Vows & Vengeance

Cupcakes & Corpses

Tea Leaves & Troubled Spirits

Haunted Honeymoon

Wedding Bells & Psychic Spells

Phantoms Are Forever

*Skeletons & Scandals (featuring Cooking With Ghosts:
Hauntingly Good Southern Recipes)*

Murder & Marigolds (Coming Spring 2026)

**Listen to the series on the Eleven Reader
Publishing App!**

For Nyx's haunted recipes, check out Cooking With Ghosts:
Hauntingly Good Southern Recipes

Standalone Cozy Mystery

The Purrfectly Haunted Library

Sister Witches of Story Cove Series

Cinder

Belle

Snow

Ruby

Zelle

Sister Witches of Story Cove Complete Set

***

Witchy Candy Shop Mysteries

Tricks and Treats

Candy and Creeps

Gum and Ghouls

VISIT MY STORE

Did you know you can buy directly from me? When you do, the retailer doesn't take a cut and I can pass on the savings to YOU!

https://mistyevansbooks.com/shop

Benefits:

You can find ALL my books in one place

SAVE money

EARLY access to new releases

Special Collections, Boxed eSets, and Limited Editions

Support a small business (and support a dream!)

Why Buy Direct?

When you purchase a book by your favorite author, electronic or print, on retailer platforms, the company keeps 30-70% of the sale, leaving the author with little to no profit (after the company deducts delivery fees, taxes, and other fees).

Buying directly from the author means that more goes to them so they can keep turning out stories for you. Every published story, every book, requires cover art, editing, and hours and hours of the author's time simply to create it. Not to mention overhead costs, such as websites, newsletters, writing software, graphics programs, advertising, taxes, etc.

In addition, one of the big-name retailers requires exclusivity, and all of them have terms of service and rules and regulations that make it challenging and time-consuming for an indie author to navigate the publishing world.

Most of us would MUCH rather spend our time creating more stories for YOU, rather than trying to jump through the hoops at the retailers. Buying direct from your favorite authors (where available) helps ensure that an author you love is not subject to unexplained account closures, withholding of royalties, censorship, and other issues that can affect their livelihood.

I've experienced ALL of these. By buying direct, you help put control of my work back in my hands - and I can continue to write more.

Either way, thank you for supporting me! I understand buying direct doesn't work for everyone and even if you use the retailers to buy my books, I appreciate you!

Happy reading,

Misty

https://mistyevansbooks.com/shop

**Don't want to miss a single release? Sign up for my
newsletter at www.mistyevansbooks.com**

Black Swan Division Romantic Thriller Series

Redeeming Meg

Tempting Tessa

Avenging Jessie

SEALs of Shadow Force Series

Fatal Truth

Fatal Honor

Fatal Courage

Fatal Love

Fatal Vision

Fatal Thrill

Risk

**Listen to the series on the Eleven Reader
Publishing App!**

—

SEALS of Shadow Force Series: Spy Division

Man Hunt

Man Killer

Man Down

Covert Affairs

Covert Tactics

Covert Obsession

**Listen to the series on the Eleven Reader
Publishing App!**

The SCVC Taskforce Series

Deadly Pursuit

Deadly Deception

Deadly Force

Deadly Intent

Deadly Affair, A SCVC Taskforce novella

Deadly Attraction

Deadly Secrets

Deadly Holiday, A SCVC Taskforce novella

Deadly Target

Deadly Rescue

Deadly Bounty

Deadly Betrayal

Deadly Threat

The Super Agent Series

Operation Sheba

Operation Paris

Operation Proof of Life

Operation Lost Princess

Operation Ambush

Operation Contraband

Operation Sleeping With the Enemy

Operation Heist

The Justice Team Series with Adrienne Giordano

Stealing Justice

Cheating Justice

Holiday Justice

Exposing Justice

Undercover Justice

Protecting Justice

Missing Justice

Defending Justice

Schock Sisters Mystery Series w/Adrienne Giordano

1st Shock

2nd Strike

3rd Tango

4th Silence

The Secret Ingredient Culinary Mystery Series

The Secret Ingredient, A Culinary Romantic Mystery with Bonus Recipes

The Secret Life of Cranberry Sauce, A Secret Ingredient Holiday Novella

MEET MISTY

USA TODAY Bestselling Author Misty Evans is celebrating her 100th published novel in 2025. She loves writing romantasy, urban fantasy, paranormal romance, and mystery/suspense. Under her pen name, Nyx Halliwell, she also writes supernatural cozy mysteries.

When not reading or writing (which is most of the time), she enjoys music, movies, and hanging out with her husband, twin sons, and three spoiled rescue dogs. She's a crafter at heart and has far too many projects to finish.

Visit www.mistyevansbooks.com to check out her online store and sign up for her newsletter.

NOTE FROM MISTY

Thank you for reading this story! It is an honor and a privilege to write books for you. I'm an indie author, and every fan is important to me. I pour my heart into each story and do my best to bring you an escape from the real world.

Readers are the key to my success - not a traditional publishing deal (I've had four), an agent (I've had two), or a publicity team (yes, you guessed it, I've had several of those as well.)

Those of you who read my books, love my characters and worlds, and then tell others about them are the best of friends. I adore you and will keep writing if you keep reading!

If you'd like to learn about my other books, sales, and special promotions, please sign up for my newsletter at **www.mistyevansbooks.com**. You'll receive FREE series starters from me.

Support me directly (no retailer taking their cut), grab special edition box sets, and get new releases before they are out at retailers by visiting my store **https://mistye vansbooks.com/shop**.

I have sales and offer NEW RELEASES early! Check it out.

Last but not least, if you enjoy clean, cozy mysteries, visit my pen name **www.nyxhalliwell.com** to see those books.

Thank you, and happy reading!

Misty